Peoples of Tomorrow

Peoples of Tomorrow

By Seth Jablon

Nagual Books

Nagual Books

Peoples of Tomorrow
Copyright © 2018 by Seth Jablon.

This book is a work of fiction.
Names, characters, businesses, organizations, places, events and incidents either are the product of the author's imagination or are used fictitiously. Any resemblance to actual persons, living or dead, events, or locales is entirely coincidental.

For information visit:
www.nagualbooks.com

Book and cover design by Seth Jablon.
Text set in Adobe Caslon Pro.

First Edition: November 2018
ISBN: 978-1-7329520-0-3

10 9 8 7 6 5 4 3 2 1

For my father, and for my son—
a person of tomorrow.

The Expedition

Chapter 1

Falling
towards Egolsia

Constant gazed out over the galaxy. The warm purple hue
that traced the opening of the wormhole crept slowly into
view at the edge of the corridor viewport. It pulsed with
a subtle iridescence as it spun about its impossibly black
center, winding and twisting with a slow, methodical swing
that seemed intent to go on forever. He never ceased to find
this display fascinating: it was like standing on the edge of a
vast body of water, watching that eternal undulation which
always possessed the ability to calm the mind.

Nevertheless Constant found himself to be quite nervous,
aimlessly shifting his weight from foot to foot. The sight of
the wormhole had enraptured him and made his pulse rise,
but the fluttering in his chest he knew came from knowing
what awaited him on the other side. Besides the obvious
scientific and personal implications of what he was about to
embark upon, his intuition was also telling him that there

was something about this expedition, something he could not precisely place, some sort of possibility that he felt like he had been preparing for his whole life.

He unconsciously squeezed the transmission in his hand that had set all of these wheels in motion. It had come from a small group of people on the distant planet to which he was now heading: Egolsia.

It was well known that Egolsia had, for a long time, been heading headlong towards a crisis in its organic and socio-logical development—one so curious that it had drawn the attention of many a scientific mind from around the galaxy—but now it appeared as if they had reached a partic-ularly critical impasse. The transmission itself was proof.

It had come from an obscure source, through a very much unofficial channel, as a final plea for assistance. Apparently, the Local Stellar Cooperative, who had for many moons been attempting to work diplomatically with the power possessors of the planet, had now decided to pull out of the planet completely. In the process, they had created the Council for the Temporary Containment of Egolsia in order to monitor their new technological embargo and sanctions on the planet, which prevented any interstellar travel. Luckily, the transmission had been passed on to Constant's people by the Council, but only as a courtesy.

Constant Zeta was, in fact, the proud offspring of over 752 generations of extraspecieologists. On his planet, the pursuit of specific studies had developed over millennia, inadvertently passing from tradition to a voluntary caste system, to the near resemblance of different races. Most of these studies were centered on the cataloging and understanding of the many cultures of all sentient beings within their local galactic region. Egolsia was one of them.

The Cooperative had selected him specially for this position not only because he was a rising star within his planet's scientific community, but also due to the fact that he possessed an extensive knowledge, almost unparalleled, of such types of planets and their respective cultures. Moreover, and more to the point, he was selected for his progressive and controversial theories as far as his contemporaries were concerned—some even considering them radical—on primitive inter-special encounters. i.e., Contact.

A mellow tone reverberated down the corridor indicating the entrance sequence had begun. His heart rate elevated further; this was his favorite part.

The ship he was traveling in belonged to a modern interstellar class. Manufactured on a neighboring planet, it was specifically designed for the scientific expeditions preferred by his homeworld. It was shaped like a very long tube, near perfectly smooth, with the exception of a series of viewports, and almost invisible bisecting seams near the front of the ship. Its construction allowed for a slow passage into a variety of wormholes through which it was accustomed to travel. As a by-product, it accommodated a large number of consecutive compartments, with varying atmospheres and compressions used for a diversity of studies. And so, because of this somewhat awkward and not-so-compact construction, the ship was equipped with two cold fusion reactors, one at each end, so that it could move into a wormhole in successive stages.

As Constant gazed with anticipated wonder, the front

part of the ship protracted out, nearly the entire length of the ship itself, dividing into three separate sections, which began to spin at different rates. The first section slowly passed into the black void at the center of the wormhole, quickly followed by the second, spinning and shooting forward out, like a key engaging a lock.

The ship itself, ironically, had been designed after an actual terrestrial worm-like organism they had found on a far reaching semi-gaseous planet. This worm moved through its surrounding gaseous space by successively protracting and contracting a section of its body at a time. It did this in a way which confounded its planet's physics and miraculously allowed it to shift ever so slightly forward and backward in time, classing it with those organisms whose forms of propulsions of flight, or in some cases very existence, remained a mystery of nature. Needless to say, it also made these worms quite difficult to catch, though one was in fact once caught for a brief period, and its study revolutionized interstellar travel in a single solar cycle.

As he contemplated this worm, an electric charge passed over the surface of his skin, waking him from his reverie—this sensation indicated what he had so patiently been waiting for—he was about to pass the horizon of the wormhole. He fought to focus his mind, as he did not want to miss the transition. This moment has a tendency to disassociate one's thoughts and separate one's consciousness, and also preceded another moment, a gap in space and time, in which there can be experienced a true state of nothingness. It was a subtle crack in the door of reality—like that pregnant moment between waking and sleep—that could be easily missed if one was not paying attention. As he prepared himself, he ran his fingers over his palms, noticing a slight perspiration.

His knees suddenly went a little weak, and his mind passed into a darkness. It was quiet there, a void, and from that darkness, a singular vision emerged. In the black around him, flecks of shining white began to twinkle about like a snowstorm. He could see a flickering of red and yellow, rising up before him like a hazy column of fire. The sight of it was blurry, as the vision itself was not completely clear, but he noted that it produced within him a profound sadness. Then, as quickly as the vision had come, it disappeared, leaving him floating once again in the darkness.

* * *

No sooner had Constant passed through the transition, than they arrived at the other side, the frontier of their destination—the Stellar 1129 system—leaving him hardly a moment to process his troubling dream. Smoothing his clothes, he collected himself, the effects of the images and emotions from the previous moment quickly dissipating. A bright and shining bell-shaped drone appeared, lifting itself from the floor to the height of his head. A small blue light blinked indicating it wished to deliver him a message. He had not noticed its silent approach, and its sudden presence startled him a bit.

"Apologies on my interruption, but your presence has been requested on the flight deck by the Captain," cooed the drone with a pristinely manufactured politeness.

"We will begin our descent to Egolsia momentarily."

"Please let him know I am on my way," replied Constant, smoothing his voice.

The drone silently complied and vanished as quickly as it had appeared.

"So it begins," Constant thought to himself, as he made his way lightly through the nearest airlock toward the forward bridge.

Chapter 2

The descent

It seemed like they had been waiting for quite some time for clearance to descend before they were finally given a definite answer: they were not being granted access at this time. Apparently, there was some sort of lockdown on the airspace around Egolsia at the moment, though it was not explained exactly why. They were however informed that they would be given alternative instructions momentarily.

From the viewport of the flight deck, Constant got his first look at the infamous planet for which he had traveled so very far, but still somehow remained just outside his grasp. Its upper sphere loomed before them, swallowing up the majority of the viewport. He was immediately struck by the fact that the famously blue planet was not so blue. A massive gray and brown swath was engulfing almost half of the visible hemisphere. It appeared to be moving as well, great plumes of clouds swelling and twisting, silently devouring what was left of the already hazy blue surface. Constant felt a sinking feeling in his chest as he realized he was witnessing some sort of catastrophic natural disaster.

He knew Egolsia had been suffering from a wildly imbalanced weather system for quite some time. From what he knew, this was primarily a by-product of their strange and unfortunate relationship with the energy sources that powered their way of life. In fact, this relationship was bound into the very fabric of their society and formed the basis of much of their ruling class's power. It had also most certainly played a role in the diplomatic breakdown that had just occurred between their power possessors and the Local Stellar Cooperative, which had in turn, provided the reason for which Constant was headed there now.

The Council for the Temporary Containment of Egolsia had, many times over, offered the Egolsians potential alternatives to their very destructive practices for generating the energy that they believed they needed. But, the Egolsians had remained stubbornly unable to hold to their promise that they would not use any such technology for the purpose of violence. Stranger than their relationship to energy was their need to use whatever technological advancements they had at their disposal to hurt and destroy each other. It was a mania that had pervaded throughout their species since their very first civilizations.

The sight of Egolsia now began to quickly swing out of view. They had been instructed to wait in orbit at the nearby Red Planet and made haste to take up their station and hopefully gain the clearance they so desperately needed to get their expedition underway.

The descent

***

The view over the Red Planet was a much different one. Its harsh desert surface spread beneath them in a broad orange arc. In the distance was Egolsia, much smaller and appearing more blue and white than before. Huge ships and dozens of smaller ones were coming and going from their immediate view—most of them departing from the Red Planet. Far below them was the city of Cydonia, burrowed deep under the Martian soil, and the center of all this activity. It was there that the Council for the Temporary Containment of Egolsia had gathered, and from there that they were waiting on word of their access.

Constant paced back and forth, discussing the situation with the Captain. Apparently, there was, in fact, a devastating storm crossing Egolsia, but that was not the reason, or at least not directly, why they were not able to descend as of yet, considering their ships could easily navigate it. More to the point was the fact that in the midst of this storm some skirmishes between two warring Egolsian tribes were reaching their climax. This, coupled with the fact that the Council was attempting to coordinate a diplomatic pullout, had led them to shut down the airspace to prevent any unnecessary complications. Such matters were not the Council's usual forte, and they were doing the best that they could.

The Council had initially formed after a series of questionable experiments had been carried out on the surface of Egolsia. In their ever furious desire to wage war, the Egolsians had figured out a way to release Solar energy in huge, destructive doses, on the scale that could be found in the interior of their own Sun. Naturally, this greatly worried their neighbors and had drawn the attention of not only the entire inter-stellar community but also a few key figures at the Galactic level as well. In response, the Galactic Dark Star Initiative had sent some of their most skilled ambassadors to help the Local Stellar Cooperative contain the situation—lest something catastrophic befall them all.

The problem with these experiments and their subsequent application was that they released a tremendous and poisonous amount of energy into the atmosphere of Egolsia, injuring its inhabitants, other life-forms, and disturbing the delicate processes of organic life itself. The potential for disaster extended far beyond the surface of their own planet though. These explosions caused unpredictable eddies in the energy flows of the local system, not to mention that they also created the potential for chain reactions which could be disastrous for nearby solar systems.

The Council arranged a number of diplomatic missions, all failing at their central goal of convincing the leaders of Egolsia to abandon their experiments and dismantle the destructive devices and power sources they had built as a result of them. These missions spanned several generations of leadership on Egolsia, each refusing to cooperate, each finding a new variety of justifications until finally, the Council gave them an ultimatum: either disarm or be left to their own devices. They choose the latter.

And so in response, the council had effectively grounded the Egolsians—which was largely symbolic, as they simply had been unable to develop the technology to take them very far beyond their own atmosphere. Moreover, the Council had placed a very strict technological embargo on their planet, to prevent any imported technologies from aiding them in their practice of destroying each other, or of possibly disturbing any other neighboring species.

Constant and the Captain watched as the last of the ships made their departure. It was quite a sight. Some of the traffic they assumed was merely passing through. Egolsia and the surrounding area was also home to a number of wormholes, including the much more expansive Senton-12, through which they had passed on their way here. This alone brought a number of inter-galactic and inter-dimensional travelers, in addition to those who were there for diplomatic or otherwise scientific purposes.

The presence of these wormholes had in fact made Egolsia an ideal location for the construction of a wormhole mapping station. Many species had come together to build it, including some of Constant's ancestors, in their tireless pursuit of finding and studying other species, making it one of the most diverse and sophisticated stations in the system. The facility was located offshore, at a fair depth under the planet's ocean surface, not far from an area that the locals called "French Polynesia." And it was to this very station that Constant was now headed.

They did not have to wait much longer for their clearance to descend. They secured their ship in broad orbit around the Red Planet and departed in a shuttle headed at last to the increasingly tumultuous surface of Egolsia.

* * *

As they descended, Constant pressed himself against the viewport, raptly observing the slowly enlarging body. He was overwhelmed with the sight of the eagerly anticipated, and so very infamous, blue planet. His heart fluttered with a million emotions, as often happens when one has finally reached the place they have only dreamt of. He was elated beyond words to now finally see it with his own eyes.

His first impulse was only to be overwhelmed by its natural beauty, which was now becoming more and more recognizable as their ship fell quietly through soft layers of cloud formations. Grand swatches of green and blue emerged, becoming more and more vivid as craggy verdant hills, broad valleys, and vast expanses of shimmering blue water. They then passed into scenes of immense gray mountains, to the desert ranges of the southern hemisphere, and finally to the wide, ample ocean where his destination was located. Now, as they closed in, the water seemed to swallow the entire horizon in an eternal blue.

Egolsia looked so peaceful from this vantage point. This was all in sharp contrast to its reputation, however, which Constant knew quite well. It was this reputation in fact that had intrigued him the most about the premise of coming here to test his progressive theory on Contact. It would also be here that he would test his mettle as an extraspecieologist and a scientist. If he succeeded here, his theory would be all but proven within his field. As he neared the surface of the water, he pondered the fact that he did not exactly know yet what this place truly had to offer him, and had only a theoretical idea of what he had to offer it, but he was nonetheless eager to find out.

The blue finally swallowed the entirety of the viewport, and without a sound, they plunged beneath the surface, to the vast ocean deep below.

* * *

The ship glided down through the wide, blue mist, and soon a warm, glowing, conical light emerged from the obscurity of the deep ocean floor below. As they drew closer, it revealed itself to be a large glass dome which sat atop a broad bell-shaped construction situated at the center of a series of smaller similar structures that composed the sub-oceanic mapping station.

They docked at a long appendage that telescoped out to them as they approached and entered the station. They made their way through a series of airlocks, which all seemed very tedious to Constant as he was quite eager to meet the beings whose interest had caused him to travel so very far. Shaking off a brief chill from the decompression of the final airlock, Constant made his way out into the vestibule of the station.

They were immediately greeted by a small group of people, ahead of which marched a large rotund humanoid man, presumably Egolsian by his garb, waving his arms and shining with a jovial smile that had lit up as soon as he had seen Constant come through the door.

He was dressed in a long, draping blue waistcoat and

gown, with a huge, pluming scarf tied around his neck, atop which sat a beaming, ruddy face. Across his forehead protruded some sort of thin metal fin, probably an implant, and crowning around his head were shocks of black and silver hair flaring and flagging out from the sides of his impressive dome, almost seeming to wave in much the same fashion as his welcoming arms.

"Welcome, Dr. Zeta! Welcome, welcome to Earth!" boomed the barreling man, as he grabbed Constant's right hand and squeezed it. "I'm Ambassador Able. Jolly good to meet you. Come, come," he invited, laughing cheerfully.

Constant politely ignored the inaccuracy of the title the Ambassador had given him. They had no such designators in his society—by Egolsian standards, everyone on his planet would be considered a doctor by virtue of their education—but he understood this was merely a sign of respect, and so he just smiled and nodded in acknowledgment.

"Ambassador, thank you," replied Constant politely in his well studied, but mostly unpracticed, Egolsian English.

"Come, come," he said again, taking his arm gingerly. Constant had immediately noticed his large rotund body as he had entered the room but was now surprised how lightly he moved, as if like a dancer. He effortlessly guided him over to the small group of people that had remained behind him.

"Doctor! At the risk of overwhelming you after your long trip—well, some of us are just dying to meet you…"

Constant knew enough of English idioms to know that none of them were in fact "dying," still that phase seemed comical to him. He smiled inwardly.

The descent

As he surveyed the rest of the politely silent group, he was struck right away by one person in particular, whose presence seemed to leap forward from the rest. It was a woman. She was fashioned with darkly cropped hair and possessed the most bright blue eyes. She had pink and blue geometric shapes either painted or tattooed over them, and wore an all white asymmetrical jumpsuit, crisscrossed with folds of fabric, and with a short raised hood that slightly obscured her visage. She stepped forward and introduced herself, pushing her hood back to reveal the full measure of her elegantly fierce face.

"Hello, Dr. Zeta," she said extending her hand. "It's a pleasure to meet you—I am Dr. Whitney. I've heard so much about you. We're all so grateful you could make it all the way here. I am so eager to hear your ideas." Constant gently took her hand and embraced it, as he knew was custom.

"It would make me most happy to do so Dr. Whitney. I shall study that I am able," Constant replied with a cordial smile. He met her gaze, which she returned then shyly looked away.

The Ambassador proceeded to introduce him to the rest of the salutation heavy group before he and his team were quickly whisked away to their quarters. As they made their way, Constant's thoughts returned to the woman he had just met.

He knew from his extensive travels and interactions with other species, that it was not so much the ones with wildly different bodies that were a shock to meet, but rather those who had nearly identical bodies, yet with minor differences. Constant himself very much resembled the Egolsian Nordic, though a bit taller, and with shock white hair. He was definitely taken with Dr. Whitney's piercing blue eyes, as his own were—like all of his people's—a smoldering orange. All the same, although he was aware that her semblance had taken him, he was also sure that he had detected something else in her presence that he had not expected to find here—some awareness, some depth of purpose, something that he had seen behind those eyes.

Chapter 3

Briefing
at the sub-oceanic
mapping station

The next morning Constant arranged for his team, who had arrived ahead of him, to receive a pre-mission briefing from their station contact. Having a little extra time beforehand, he had agreed to take a guided tour of the station with one of its staff who had seemed as eager to expound its inner workings as Constant was to learn of them.

Walking the halls with his guide, he was immediately struck by the diversity of its inhabitants as they moved in and out of his view, intently engaged in the activities of the day. Some of the species were quite well known to him, such as many of the humanoid ones that often worked in cooperation with his own. Then there were others that he did not immediately recognize, but knew of their stellar relations. Some more he knew of but had never seen before, and still a few further that he did not even know existed.

He passed a rare species of evolved bird, who bore no resemblance to any species in his mental repertoire. It wore red plumes on its forehead, had large opal eyes, and gestured gregariously with its wings as it conversed with a colleague. He also saw what he believed was commonly called a Mono-be—another creature that he had never seen before, yet still heard of despite its obscurity. It was shaped like a sphere, covered in sleek silvery fur, and it propelled itself by effortlessly gliding along the floor, making for quite a curious sight. As it passed close by, he became flustered and nearly stepped on it. After that encounter, he made sure to stay present to what was underfoot as they further made their way through the station's vast corridors.

As they went, he observed that all these species seemed engaged in their work in a way that gave them an air of obliviousness to each other, as if whatever they were doing there was the most important thing on the station. He knew that many of them did, in fact, cooperate with each other, yet still, they all seemed to carry on with no second thought to the fact that the species which populated the planet on which they were currently stationed was approaching a near cataclysmic crisis.

That was not an entirely fair assessment though, he pondered, as some of those species had been studying on the planet for thousands of years. The mapping station alone had been there for two Egolsian millennia, and many of those species had lived there their entire lives, some even for generations.

In fact, some of Constant's ancestors, he had been told in

his pre-departure briefing, had helped in its conception, as well as its construction.

It was a beautifully simple and timeless design, his guide expounded to him as they made their way into a massive grand hall. The station itself was built like an interstellar craft, and could even be converted to one if necessary, his guide explained. It was shaped like a large smooth partially flattened bell, with a swollen center, and a glass peak at the top. Contained within the peak was a large observation deck, which was centered on a narrow luminous shaft that connected to the reactor deep below. Thus, they could flood the surrounding water with light, since they were at a depth to which very little sunlight reached. It also created the most welcoming, homey glow as you approached it with your ship, his guide added wistfully. Constant agreed.

His guide continued to dissect the station in all its great minutia as they walked through the grand hall and the many corridors that radiated out from its cavernous center. In total, layered down from the observation deck to its bottommost base, there were 27 levels, grouped and subdivided for the research facilities and living quarters of the station's inhabitants. The bottom levels were reserved for the permanent mooring or temporary docking of spacecraft, and the living and meeting quarters for visitors.

Constant's scientific curiosity had been piqued by a number of studies his guide had explained were going on at the station's myriad facilities, but the one in particular that interested him the most was the central system that ran the mapping instruments, which formed the primary purpose of this station. He asked his guide if they had enough time for a tour. He at first seemed reticent to skip directly ahead to what was probably his grand finale, but then quickly transitioned to the excitement of being able to explain its fascinating inner workings to yet another newcomer.

They made their way to a glass lift that vertically traced the walls of the massive central atrium. They soared over twenty levels in but a few moments, producing in Constant a dizzying sensation that he accounted not so much to the lift's speed, but to the fact that the compartment that they were in was nearly invisible. Through the floor, he watched the tops of the non-deciduous, exotic trees that encircled the bottommost level grow smaller and smaller. As they continued to ascend, they passed tiers upon tiers of foreign greenery, which was no doubt there to supplement the generation of breathable gases for a number of species, and also to comfort the inhabitants in this home so far from their own.

They reached the uppermost level and exited out into the antechamber of the room that contained the mapping system. This was as far as the two could proceed, as the room itself was sealed. "Room" was really an unsuitable word as it spanned the entirety of that floor, and was as tall as several levels combined. The only way to view the contents of the space was through a wide, narrow window, more like a slit, seamlessly covered by a panel his guide was now sliding back by hand. Constant stooped down, as the observation window was obviously designed for a caretaker much smaller in stature than him, and as his guide narrated, he peered inside.

At first it seemed as if his eyes simply needed adjustment

to the difference in light, as the image he saw was quite stark, almost graphic. There were only two visible colors in the room—white and black. The contents of the room also appeared to be as spartan. He saw rows and rows of tall, flat, massive and severely geometric obelisks. They were all black, impossibly black it seemed as if no light were able to reflect off of them. They all stood in, from what Constant was able to estimate, a shallow pool of glassy black liquid, which covered the entirety of the floor. This was in stark contrast to the walls, which were an almost impossible white and seemed to glow with a soft, radiant light.

Constant's guide explained how the arrangement acted as an organically-networked molecular subsystem within which an almost infinite amount of knowledge and data could be stored. It was, in fact, alive; an organic-based neuron-transmission system, a living organism, a mind. It was sentient to a degree, but only on the level of say, a plant-based organism. It was much like a brain, but not the entirety of a brain, simply a portion of it. And it functioned like one too, with electrical impulses interfacing with myriad other impulses and nodes that occurred on a molecular level.

It had been designed to store all of the inter-dimensional connections (i.e., wormholes) within the Galactic neighborhood in which they now resided, and to process probabilities and outcomes, distances and potential pathways of travel, and to even fold points in space. However, it could not actually think for itself. There was that type of intelligent technology on the station, but it was kept carefully separated from this system for ethical reasons.

The data the system contained was, by its nature, fluid. Its contents were much like an astronomical map, only focused on the negative space around it, and the changing intersections within it. It contained recordings of wormhole coordinates and conditions, updates and observations from other systems, as well as prognostications on where and when new wormholes could appear, and when known ones might cease to be.

What actually existed on the sub-molecular level of the system, whatever it was that had been grown and "crystallized" in order to store this data, was a subject of much debate and speculation. There existed a theorem—of which there was a considerable amount of evidence—that suggested the organic substructures that had been cultivated so as to interlace themselves into the ever-changing networks that were needed for this task, were in fact, not only alive on the level of plant matter, and even mimicking the neurological mappings of the brain, but were in fact the actual buildings, homes, and bodies of an entire civilization and race of subatomic beings. It was a world unto its own, populated by those whose lives and daily activities were synonymous with the transmission and storage of said data.

There was a great deal of controversy over this matter; that is, whether it was ethical to effectively "enslave" an entirely unknown species, without their consent, albeit for the noble pursuit of interstellar travel, even if they had been brought into existence solely for this purpose. It was true that this work benefited a nearly incalculable number of species, and though the purpose of this world ostensibly acted for this theoretically subatomic civilization as their origin story and meaning of life, its operation still persisted without their express consent, and possibly without knowledge, all together. And so, it had its staunch critics and stalwart proponents equally measured on both sides.

The solution to this controversy eventually came from one of the system's original designers, now in his old age. At his instruction, they installed an electron-based molecular-atomic interface port that cued directly to the communications grid of the system. This was a means for these beings, if they did in fact exist and should become aware of their purpose, to send a message directly to their creators in acquiescence or denial of their essential task. They would then be provided with permanent extradition if they so desired it.

Constant's guide held his wrist to his ear. Constant was apparently being called into attendance to the briefing that was being held on the observation deck directly above them. His team had already arrived, and their station liaison, who happened to also be the station's chief engineer, was en route. His guide gracefully concluded their tour and saw him swiftly to the lift.

* * *

As Constant stepped out into the great volume of space that was the observation deck, he immediately noticed his team who were gathered on a set of low circular couches positioned in the center of the room. He strode over to them, beaming a morning smile.

They had all seemed tiny from where he had first entered

the room. He did not realize how large the massive glass dome that sat atop the deck was. It had seemed so small and delicate from the viewport of his ship, but now that he saw it in comparison with his crew, he realized it was actually several stories tall, and composed most of the volume of the very large space he was now in. His team seemed as taken with it as he was, and they all stood there transfixed at the dark and mysterious ocean, with its glowing sea creatures that danced in illumination just outside the glass walls. They were snapped from their reverie as Constant approached and rose to happily greet him.

It was a small group, as he had intentionally kept his team trim and to-the-point. Partly because this was, after all, an off-the-record expedition, and moreover he was a subscriber to the theory that fewer members make a stronger and more focused team, especially for what he had assumed was going to be a challenging and nuanced undertaking. And so, he had brought his two most essential and trusted colleagues, as well as one new addition, making only three members in total: Bright Theta, a fellow Elayday countryman, his assigned assistant and diplomatic support, Stantish Harr, his longtime colleague and strategic advisor, and Owvi, a close friend and his chief engineer.

Bright was the newest member of his team. He resembled Constant, even by his home world's standards, with his bright white shock hair and tall, slender physique, only he was twenty-six solar cycles (amounting to roughly 200 Egolsian years) younger than Constant, who was already considered somewhat young for such an undertaking. Bright was, as his name would suggest, quite intelligent and showed much promise, though by the standards of such a great peregrination in which they were now involved, troublingly young. He had been assigned by the Elayday Science Fellowship to assist and learn from Constant, a bit to Constant's chagrin, thus ensuring a fresh familiarization of a still relativity misunderstood species by a new generation. It had been the Fellowship's only request, and in lieu of any other bureaucratic oversight, Constant had gracefully consented.

Stantish on the other hand, he had known for quite some time. He came from a neighboring system whose tribes often worked closely with his own on a variety of such expeditions. Physically, he had a similar stature as Constant, save for his blue-black hair, which was pulled tightly back into a series of intricate knots at the back of his head. He bore a tribal tattoo, which traced a thin line down the center of his face, marked off at parabolic intervals. He fashioned himself in a lightweight jumpsuit like Constant's, popular for these types of expeditions, only it was dyed black instead of dark blue, and intricately embroidered with the symbolic red thread of his people.

He came from a tribe famous for strategy and inter-species relations. They were by nature a martial people but had long since evolved past their war-like tendencies, which, over eons, had ultimately made them experts in peace-keeping. They did, however, celebrate their heritage once a year with a grand ceremonial battle. All the adult men and women participated in this for the purpose of remembering and reflecting upon their roots, and to help "keep their blood red and on the inside" as they would say. It rarely resulted in any fatalities, and when it did, there was no regret, as to die partaking in the "Great Fight" was considered a most profound honor.

Owvi was his third team member, and one of his closest friends. Constant had met Owvi on another expedition many years ago and had become immediately attached to him. Owvi was a descendant of the Wvio; a highly intelligent species which had evolved from a sea born organism, much like the inhabitants of Egolsia had, though one of a much different carbon composition. He had a stout body, almost geometrically arranged, with a barrel-like torso, short legs and long tube-like arms which terminated into a series of delicate fingers. His whole body was smooth, tan and covered with a fine, soft down hair. Atop it sat a well-formed but quite bulbous head with large, perfectly circular, particularly gentle, deep brown eyes. Below them, punctuating his face, was a small delicate mouth. Partly because of the Wvio's great capacity for empathy, they had long since evolved the capacity for telepathy, and over the millennia, their mouths had shrunk as if in response. In addition to their empathetic nature, they had brilliant, almost machine-like intellects, which made them excellent engineers, and a natural choice for this type of expedition.

Besides, Constant thought as he approached the group, he held quite an affection for Owvi, and just liked being around him. Something about the composition of his body, he mused, gave him a near irresistible desire to squeeze him.

As Constant greeted his team, Chief Officer Fair, the station liaison, entered through an adjacent corridor.

They had spoken briefly over a communications link

before Constant's descent, and so since he had been most eager to meet him.

"Greetings Constant Zeta!" shouted Fair as he hurried toward him with arms extended. "I pray your journey was a lesson!"

"And yours," replied Constant both grasping the other's forearms.

"Come—," he said gesturing towards a low circular bench, "—let us talk."

* * *

The group took their places on the bench after exchanging the customary pleasantries and introductions. Constant, eager to begin, started the discussion directly.

"Officer Fair, what is our first step here?" Constant asked.

Fair paused and looked around at the group.

"Unfortunately, there has been a slight change in plans since we last spoke—the situation has progressed here, or rather, deteriorated since you departed. Tomorrow, Ambassador Able and Dr. Whitney will escort you to a summit being held at a cooperative Egolsian base located in a southwestern territory of the northern continent. There you will present your proposal to an adjunct committee, who have been collected there to host diplomatic talks."

Constant knit his brow. His heart was anxiously swelling as to what was to come next.

"I thought the purpose of this expedition was to pursue avenues outside of the present channels, and that was mainly because diplomacy has already been exhausted by the Council?" he asked.

"Yes, yes, it is true," Fair replied. "This, however, is a different group. As you will no doubt see, things do not always go according to plan here. And you have to remember all the stellar nations that have been involved here for so many years—it was not our decision, nor was it Ambassador Able or Dr. Whitney's, but the Ambassador has assured me that this will not change our course, only supplement it. It will allow this new cooperative simply to be kept abreast of it."

"Who will be attending this meeting?" asked Stantish.

"I do not have a list of all of the attendees, but I have been told there will be a representative of the Dark Star Initiative there, as well as a member of the Temporary Council of the Containment of Egolsia, along with a few of the sympathetic Egolsian leaders that we had planned on coordinating with," Fair replied tentatively.

"Very well," Constant conceded with notable reservation.

"You see, the state of affairs has worsened here," Fair continued, "and a few members of the Council thought it best if some coordination took place. I am afraid to say, that the situation here is becoming quite untenable."

"How do you mean?" Constant asked. "I thought we were already in a state of urgency, and that was the impetus of this final expedition?"

"Yes, yes, but it was a slow moving one, and now its pace has quickened. Please, let me explain—"

Fair proceeded to lay out the current conditions, as best he could, while Constant and his team listened and took note, exchanging glances along the way. Fair himself was not directly part of this expedition but had been asked to act as a liaison between Constant's team and the Egolsian team here on the ground. In Constant's few exchanges, he had found Fair to be eager to help and forthwith with useful information, and so, Constant considered his assessment of the situation as valuable as one of his team members. And so, he listened intently.

Previously, Fair began, everyone had at least been talking, and now they were not talking at all. In addition to this, he explained, the situation had become more complicated in the following ways: as they knew, the entire expedition had been arranged in a very non-official manner, though many who were in the need-to-know did, in fact, know about it, including key parts of the North American Egolsian leadership. It had been done so somewhat quietly by a small group of scientists, emissaries, and a few key people in the Cabinet of Extra-Terrestrial relations, of which Ambassador Able was one of the last remaining members. This group—which had now been formally dissolved after negotiations had broken down—and a small sympathetic constituency of the Local Stellar Cooperative and The Temporary Council of the Containment of Egolsia, were all that composed the small force that had made this expedition possible.

This group hadn't exactly included their respective councils. They had simply informed them and then taken their lack of opposition as approval. To be fair, this was the entire point. The formal channels, what few there were, had either completely shut down, or were purposely severed, and so now the expedition that had never been formally arranged, could neither officially proceed, nor be officially terminated.

This was primarily because the agencies they had made arrangements with simply no longer existed. And secondly, as Fair had previously stated, no one was communicating. Even as they spoke, council members were leaving the planet—the Cooperative had shored itself up on the Red Planet to discuss their future position on Egolsia.

Clearly, this was not good. There was still hope that the expedition might be able to proceed, Fair reiterated cautiously, but this hope balanced wholly on a fruitful dialogue with the summit the following day. Constant, concerned but exceedingly determined, nodded his head in agreement. He was still eager for the opportunity to prove himself, and to see his theories finally tested. Moreover, he was optimistic that there was still some sympathy left for the fate of the Egolsian people. They would have to see what fortune the stars held for them tomorrow.

Chapter 4

An unexpected influence

Constant scheduled for them to leave as early as possible for the summit the following morning. He was the first to arrive at the launch bay and spent his last remaining hour there prepping his team. Despite his disquietude about the endeavors of the day, he pressed one of the station engineers to give him a brief exposition on the vessel that they would be traveling in.

The ship had caught his attention as it was designed by the same makers of the mapping station—and was precisely the kind that so interested the Egolsians. From the outside, it was a smooth, silver disc, gracefully swelling in the center to a height half its width, and topped with a blue glass dome. Inside, it opened out into a large, raised circular hall, which was encircled by a series of intricate corridors and staterooms used for longer voyages. Elevated above the hall was the flight deck, and situated under the top dome and below the hall at the center of the ship, was the reactor.

The reactor was cold fusion, much like the ones on the ship he had traveled here on and was capable of interstellar travel. However, this model used an older and less accessible element in its reaction, and also made use of a series of gyrating magnetic spheres embedded into the interior circumference, which allowed for a finer pitch and yaw, making the craft extremely nimble.

Like all interstellar vessels, the reactor itself did not specifically create propulsion, as the Egolsians had so fruitlessly hypothesized in their attempt to reverse engineer them, but quite conversely created a relative gravity field, into which the ship simply "fell." This, combined with the alloy out of which the hull of the vessel was constructed, allowed it to move at near stellar speeds, turn at perpendicular angles, and pass through any atmosphere—or liquid for that matter—with near zero friction so as to hardly make even a wave. It was precisely this kind of technology that the Egolsians were forbidden to have.

Promptly at the hour of departure, Ambassador Able and Dr. Whitney arrived at the launch bay. Constant had not seen Dr. Whitney since their first meeting, and as soon as she walked in, he noticed his heart give a strange leap. He was struck by this and did not know exactly how to categorize what he was feeling, though, admittedly, the sensations and emotions were fairly clear. He was attracted to her.

Being learned on so many cultures and the inter-relations of such a broad range of species—and subsequently their sexual relations and practices of courtship—had made him fairly versed in the myriad forms of sexual impulses, especially as they related to the attraction between species. He had never experienced it first hand, at least not to the degree he believed he was experiencing it now, save of course for the occasional passing sensation. This felt different.

He knew the draw between species could range from simple curiosity to, in some cases, a quite intense inducement. He was not sure exactly why this was the case—perhaps some primal instinctive impulse to expand and improve the gene pool beyond the planet of one's own arising, or perhaps it was that stimulus born of a contrast between the familiar and unfamiliar that was erotic—but he did not believe that it was merely this that was at the bottom of his magnetism to Dr. Whitney. He felt something for her.

Constant was snapped back into the moment by an introduction to one of Officer Fair's engineers. He was going to captain their ship and act as an envoy, making all of the appropriate introductions to the committee. The group gathered for a moment to exchange pleasantries and briefly review the flight plan, before they boarded the ship and began the departure sequence.

The ship glided into an adjacent compartment, which was then sealed and flooded before a second lock was opened, releasing the ship gracefully into the surrounding waters. As the captain paused there to orient their flight path, Constant took a last look at the mapping station through the dome of the flight deck. He watched the glow emitting from the glass top of the observatory, and marveled how it illuminated so many of the unusual sea creatures that floated blissfully and obliviously by. The whole scene created an unexpected melancholy in Constant. He experienced a strange premonition that this would be the last time he would see it.

The ship departed at a rapid speed, though Constant would hardly have noticed if he had not been looking out the window. The captain had left the dome transparent for them to view the outside, though at this point, because of the speed at which they were traveling, it was only a blur of blue.

A short time passed, and the captain announced that they were nearing the North American coast, and so would now be going airborne in order to reach the base located in the New Mexico desert. In a flash, they were hovering high enough above Egolsia to see the graceful curve of its far edges. They paused just long enough for Constant to peer out of the dome and take in the most wonderful view. The Egolsian Sun was breaking day on the eastern side of the continent, splashing cool morning rays over its wild green forests, patchwork fields, and swirling clouds. And then, just as suddenly as they had risen, they descended, stopping quite abruptly not very far above the surface. They were hovering above a vaguely circular patch of ground in the middle of a vast desert. They waited there for a few moments while the captain exchanged words with another voice through a long tube that extended from the console.

Taking the opportunity of this pause, the envoy began explaining their brief itinerary. As the captain switched switches and pressed nondescript buttons, he told them that the place where they would be going to speak with the committee was a meeting space in an extraterritorial conference facility, adjacent to a nearby, much larger underground cooperative base.

Constant had heard of this place—and not for encouraging reasons—and so he had immediately become wary when he learned that the conference would be taking place there. Shrouded in secrecy, so little was actually known about what went on at the facility, and until this very moment, Constant was not sure that it had actually existed. Its reputation was clouded in mostly rumor and hearsay, and its activities were described as ranging from the more sinister to the more predictable and scientifically mundane. Most of the stories, however, were troublingly oriented around genetic experimentation, and practices which some described as "mental warfare." These subjects Constant found distasteful and uninteresting: it was not what was considered in his society "good science." And if what he had heard was any indication of truth, he wanted no part of it.

The facility did however obviously exist, and it appeared that it was, at least for now, definitely being used for cooperative purposes. Constant was told that it possessed an extraterritorial conference center, and it was there that they would meet with the committee. It was not clear why they would need an extraterritorial conference space though, and this troubled him. In his experience, such places were usually used in highly combative situations as a neutral place to host peace talks between warring civilizations, and he did not see how any of that pertained to the current situation on Egolsia.

All this passed through Constant's mind, as a large circular section of the patch of desert below them sunk slowly into the ground. Their craft gently descended into the hollow passage and was then guided into a massive underground hanger. They disembarked their ship and exited the hanger out into a central corridor. There was no ceremony upon their arrival. After only a few words exchanged by the envoy and an armed sentry, they were quietly led away to a room where they would wait for the committee to assemble.

On their largely silent walk there, Constant experienced a starkly contrasted impression to the one he had of the mapping station. There was not a buzz and a cheer here, but a tension, a guardedness, a gloom. He was happy when they finally arrived at their private waiting area. He let his breath out as they entered into the sparse room.

Constant and his team exchanged few words as they waited, each running possible dialogues in their heads. Surprisingly, they did not have to entertain themselves long and were soon escorted to the meeting room. As they approached the door, Constant felt an uncharacteristic nervousness—his palms were slightly sweaty, he felt somewhat uncomfortable in his clothes, straightening them as he went—he simply didn't know what to expect behind that door.

* * *

Upon entering, Constant felt an immediate sense of relief as he saw that the committee was much smaller than he had anticipated. On the heels of that relief, however, he was hit with a flurry of many other contradictory emotions as his eyes focused in on the figure at the center of the group. It was an Arcturian.

The Arcturians were a race whose name was quite familiar in his homeworld, as it was to most evolving civilizations, though many could go their whole lives without ever meeting one. Constant had seen one before, visiting the elders on his planet, but he had never personally met one face to face. The Arcturian had an extremely slender body, with a very large, but graceful head with deep glassy black, almond-shaped eyes, and an almost soothing light green skin tone. He also bore one of the kindest faces Constant had ever seen. There was a beauty to the Arcturian, but more impressive still was his countenance—there was an air to him that was like that of a high priest, with a piercing intelligence to match. He gracefully rose from where he sat and motioned Constant to come forward.

Constant moved to meet him with a reverent speed.

"Your Honor," he said as he stopped to bow slightly.

"Constant Zeta, it is a pleasure to finally meet you," the Arcturian replied, as if he knew all about him and had been waiting for a long time to speak with him. " I am A Huumus Sol. Please sit so we may make our introductions."

As they took their places at the ring shaped table, Owvi quickly waddled up to the Arcturian, bowed, and nearly ran back to take his seat. Able and Whitney both shot Constant inquisitive glances, to which he nodded back as if to say: "It's OK—let us see how it goes."

"Friends," A Huumus began abruptly. "I am aware that it

was unexpected for you to meet with us here, and we will reach the point shortly—but allow me first to introduce to you the rest of this council. Please know Halive Oonzidor, representative of the Dark Star Initiative, whom I have asked to join me for a series of diplomatic talks which we will also be hosting here," he said gesturing to a striking female humanoid on his left. She had a long, sweeping narrow face, dark, nearly all black eyes, flower yellow skin and woody dark hair that was finely braided down her back. She nodded and softly hummed a beautiful, almost insect-like tone, in acknowledgment.

"Please know Brave Forth," gesturing now to his right, "member of The Temporary Council of the Containment of Egolsia, whom I have also asked to be here," indicating a small, darkly handsome man with inky black coiffure, wearing a sharp Egolsian suit. Flanking him were—by their appearance and demeanor—two native Egolsians. One was a beautiful brown skinned woman wearing a tall head-dress and ceremonial garb, who was introduced as Princess Fatima. The other was a very old, very frail, gray-skinned man with ashen hair and a wizened face who maintained, it turned out for the rest of their encounter, a pallid silence. Constant and his team reciprocated the group with their own introductions, and after the normal pleasantries were exchanged, Huumus politely commenced the meeting.

"Friends, Time awaits," he enjoined. He scanned the faces in the room before he turned to Halive Oonzidor and gestured to her the floor. Halive straightened herself and gracefully began.

"Constant, I shall be direct. We are fully informed

about your expedition and the request of the Local Stellar Cooperative that prompted it. Unfortunately, the circumstances here on Egolsia have changed since you departed, and your services will no longer be needed."

There was palpable silence in the room. Constant sat stunned, not sure how to respond. A Huumus turned a sympathetic gaze. Finally, Constant broke the silence and replied with a slightly trembling voice.

"Your Honor, Councilor Oonzidor, it was my understanding that we were to present our plans to you as a courtesy, had you any insight or objections, otherwise we were to proceed outside formal channels, as it was needed for this state of, well emergency. I must admit I am at a loss for how to respond," Constant asserted. His eyes scanned the rest of the panel, looking for any reciprocation. "What of the Egolsian leadership I was set to work with? Where do they stand on this?"

"I am afraid they no longer are in a position to be of service either," Councilor Oonzidor replied evenly. "I regret to inform you that as of yesterday, a number of them have been forcibly separated from their bodies, and those that remain on the planet are no longer in a position of power. There was an attempted military coup last night. It was mostly unsuccessful, but the governmental agencies of the North American Continent have now splintered. We are bordering on chaos here."

He shot a glance to Dr. Whitney and Ambassador Able, who were exchanging their own confused glances. "This is news to us, Dr. Zeta," Dr. Whitney replied to his look, clearly exasperated herself.

"I'm sorry, you'll have to excuse us," she hastened, addressing the council, "I think there are there some calls we need to make." The two hurriedly left the meeting room, leaving Constant and his team to another exchange of confounded looks.

A disembodied but familiar voice entered Constant's mind "I don't like this." It was Owvi, breaking his promise to not use telepathy.

Huumus smiled. "I can assure you, neither do we," he replied out loud to Owvi, continuing. "Constant, we are not here to thwart you in your efforts, only to inform you of the circumstance, which has unfortunately become too unstable for you to proceed as you had planned."

"We do however understand the desire of the Collective to have a healthy and potentially productive member of this system," Councilor Oonzidor added, "but the desire for stabilization has become secondary to the need of containing potential catastrophes."

"You see Constant, I myself am here on another matter" Huumus broke in. "Unfortunately the disintegrating situation here has, in some minds, opened the question of ownership to particular parts of this planet. A faction of OoCulay and Caltroovian Paaroid Basks are, as we speak, attempting to argue a new claim to the certain parts of subterranean Egolsia. I am here solely to prevent that. As you know, we Arcturians are interested only in protecting a species' potential for Evolution, and only intervene when an outside interest seeks to prevent that.

"Halive and Councilor Forth are here in alignment with that aim. The Dark Star Initiative has sent me to aid in that process, as well as to ensure the containment of Egolsia. Fortunately for you, these matters are not of your concern."

After a pause, a bit overwhelmed, Constant still pressed.

"With all due reverence, your Honor, the Elayday's interest here, as well as my own, have nothing to do with politics, or trade—our mission here was meant to be a humanitarian one—an experiment in Contact of a purely scientific value.

"Culture cannot exist in a war zone, Constant Zeta," Huumus replied, with a noticeable shift to grave tone. "I am sorry, but we cannot support your expedition here. You are welcome to stay as an observer, to further the knowledge of your race."

Huumus arose, indicating the end of the meeting.

As the others made their way out of the meeting room, the Princess followed.

As the council dispersed, the Princess made her way over to Constant, gesturing him aside. "Dr. Zeta! Please, may I have a word," she said smiling cordially. She had the most beautifully elegant voice which, despite his current state of consternation, took him briefly off guard.

"Dr. Zeta, I am terribly sorry for all this. You see, I was in full support your efforts here, but as you can see... If there is anything I can do for you during your remaining stay here, please let me know." She squeezed his hand and quickly followed her group out of the door.

Constant turned to Owvi. "I don't like this either."

* * *

As they exited the room, Constant gave a start. In an

adjacent corridor stood a pair of OoCulay and Paaroids Basks having a silent exchange. The sight of them made him uneasy. He assumed they were the same individuals that the council was going to be speaking with the next day, but his unease with them stemmed from a heavier place. Both species he was acquainted with, and neither had ever held any interest for him.

The Paaroids were highly intelligent and technologically advanced but had a well-deserved reputation for being decidedly aggressive, bordering on brutish. They were not exactly a martial tribe, for they did not possess the warrior's honor—or soul—but were known for their ambition and assertiveness, especially as it related to the expansion of their resources. They shared a special relation to Egolsia, as they were of reptilian descent, and their ancestors shared a similar genesis as one of Egolsia's first sentient inhabitants, a massive reptilian race. Seeing them here gave Constant a certain uneasiness.

The OoCulay he found off-putting as well. Like the Paaroids, they had been evolving for around 20 million years. The OoCulay were a distant relative, some sort of cousin of the Paaroids, but with a different origin. Physically they were quite different—instead of the tall, solid quasi-humanoid, quasi-reptilian figure, they were of an extremely slight frame, about half as tall, with a teardrop shaped head and large, ovular, glassy black eyes. They had a vague, miniature similarity to the Arcturians, but with pale almost drab gray skin, and emotionless, streamlined features.

This stoic quality was partially due to the fact that at some point during their evolution, they discovered that the experiencing of emotions was producing a deteriorating effect on their planet's atmosphere. Their planet at that time was dying, and so, as a drastic measure, they forbade any expression of emotion within its atmospheric layer. This eventually led to a culture-wide elimination of emotion, embraced even by those who had emigrated to other systems, and the many who lived on permanent expedition. There was a small faction though, who managed to escape this practice and left to colonize a fairly inhospitable planet in a neighboring system. There is little known of them after the fact, however, as they ceased all artificial and technologically based communications, and successfully petitioned the Dark Star Initiative for evolutionary asylum on religious grounds.

Shortly after this, OoCulay found themselves in another crisis. They had been proliferating for over 5 million years solely by cloning, and because of this, their DNA had begun to falter. In hopes of offsetting this degradation, they launched a several millennium long series of expeditions to seek compatible strains of DNA in the hopes of using it to strengthen their own for the reproduction of future generations. They had mainly pursued gene splicing and artificial insemination versus biological sex, as that practice had all but ceased within their culture.

Recently, however, they began to look beyond these means and pursued full physical couplings, as the lab-based experiments had given them mixed results, and in some cases, biological abominations. They had maintained a caste of females that still had their sex organs intact, and so now were exploring methods of impregnating them with less evolved, but nonetheless fresher and healthier species, through more traditional means. It was this constant search for diverse DNA that underscored the nature and quality of their current relationship with the Egolsians.

In the wake of the technological embargoes that followed Egolsia's first experiments with nuclear explosions on the surface of their planet, the OoCulay had arranged treaties with their leaders to allow for DNA and reproductive samplings of their people. These treaties allowed for the involuntary yet temporary taking of Egolsians for scientific purposes under the conditions that the specimens were first hypnotized, so as to diminish contact and destructive memories, second that they would not be physically injured, and third that they would be returned to exactly the same place they had been taken from so as to reduce the overall impact of such events.

The typical scope of their studies often focused on the examination of the reproductive systems of their specimen and was usually conducted over the course of generations in order to gather knowledge of heredity. Their specimens were often then tagged with various implants to track their movements and life patterns after they were returned.

Although they were returned with mind and body solidly intact, these same specimens were often left psychologically affected, sometimes even emotionally scarred, by the encounter. This was partly due to the invasive nature of their retrieval—often the subject was repeatedly mentally immobilized and taken from their homes in the middle of the night—but mostly due to the fact that within their primitive worldview, the beings who caused this experience should not exist at all. This gave their experiences a terrifying supernatural quality.

The OoCulay were not known for their empathy. They were highly evolved, highly intelligent beings, who looked at the Egolsians as such lesser beings that to them they resembled animals. At least, this was their general response when criticized for their treatment of some of the subjects of their experiments, and they would further argue the fact that their practices closely resembled the Egolsian's own methods of studying the animal species of their planet.

While many of these expeditions took place in rural parts of Egolsia, and though hypnosis was applied to everyone in the surrounding area, the increasing frequency of them had caused the phantasm of the OoCulay to eventually find its way into the collective consciousness and mythology of the current age of Egolsia. Ironically, this boded poorly for those that remembered their experiences, as whenever they tried to tell any of their contemporaries, they were commonly accused of mental defect, or of simply lying, and were often ostracized. It was generally accepted that the OoCulay were purely mythical, the invention of childish imaginations at best, and no matter how many incidents of contact occurred, they remained a fantastic phenomenon.

And so, knowing their complex relationship with the Egolsians—and the famous intrigue of the Paaroids— seeing them together at this precipice was unsettling to Constant, to say the least. It must be reflective of some power play that he wanted nothing to do with, he thought to himself. His journey here was not to save this world, but only to give its people another possibility.

* * *

Once they had gathered back on the ship, Constant delayed their departure to give his team an opportunity to collect themselves and discuss their next move. They all took tentative seats about the forward cabin. He surveyed the restless group.

Dr. Whitney was the first to speak. She was nearly shaking with fury; she was used to bureaucratic roadblocks and political failures, yet was still obviously nonplussed by the meeting, and so seeing one last possibility potentially slipping away, she urged Constant to stay.

"Dr. Zeta, I'm sure you are as upset by the outcome of that meeting as I am, but you have to know that there are still many of us here that desperately need your help. I assume that you are used to always doing things through their proper channels"—Constant smiled a wry smile, as she continued—"but on this planet, there is rarely a proper channel to do the right thing. Our system here is designed only to maintain itself—not to allow for ideas that could radically change things for the better." Ambassador Able nodded in agreement but hung back in a diplomatic silence.

Constant maintained his smile. "It is not your planet's official channels that concern me. I suspect that is why I was asked here to begin with. What concerns me is the word of an Arcturian."

"I agree. We have no option but to leave immediately," Bright shot out brashly, catching a side look from Constant.

"He said we could stay." Constant heard Owvi's soft words inside his head. He turned to face him.

"Owvi please, to the group—"

Owvi stepped forward, offering his velvety voice. "He said we could stay. For scientific purposes. Surely there is something of scientific value that we could be studying here."

"I believe it was clear the mission was canceled," retorted Bright. It was Owvi's turn to give him a look—one that he rarely dispensed with.

"Constant, I do believe Bright is right here. The mission we came here for was canceled," Stantish interjected, eliciting a satisfied nod from Bright. "However, if you believe there is another mission for us to undertake, I am more than willing to stay on as your security detail."

"There is still a purpose for us here yet," replied Constant. He then turned to Dr. Whitney. "Dr. Whitney, what would you have us do?"

She tentatively looked around at the group, still unsure of her footing. She took a breath and answered with assurance. "Come with me to North Dakota. There is a group of scientists and engineers there working on a number of important projects. I am sure you can help us there."

Constant nodded. It was decided. Noting Bright's unequivocal objections, Constant sent him back to the Mapping Station with the ship, so as to then rendezvous with their interstellar vessel that was still in wide orbit and await word from him there. Able indicated that he needed to attend to business in the capital and would meet them at their destination at a later date. The rest of the group prepared for departure as Dr. Whitney negotiated transportation for them. And then, as unceremoniously as they had arrived, they made their way to the exit.

* * *

They descended into a massive underground chamber carved out of bedrock, vast and mostly empty. The few vessels that were housed there varied greatly in age and sophistication. Closest to the entrance was a small number of severely shaped craft, constructed of a deep black onyx-like material he had never seen before. Nearby, parked with an ironically tight pattern for the surrounding space, were a few lozenge shaped silver and glass-clad vehicles, which looked manufactured and styled in the contemporary Egolsian fashion.

They walked quickly past these, towards the other more darkly lit end of the hall. There was a lone, angularly shaped mound, covered in a thin plastic sheet, which was in turn covered in a thick film of dust.

"It was all I could get," Dr. Whitney shrugged, as she unceremoniously removed the cover. "But should actually be just right for what we need."

The vehicle revealed beneath was something he had not anticipated. It was smaller in size than the other craft they had passed, but was much more aggressive in its appearance. It was composed primarily of a substantial, angular metal frame which suspended a boxy carriage of a different material, all punctuated by numerous rivets and shiny circular fasteners. It sat atop four massive, inflated tires, which had large, curved, blade-like protrusions, almost claw-like, that extended outwards on heavy metal shafts, strutted by gloss yellow springs.

In some ways it resembled the antique style of the vehicles he had seen before, which were still the Egolsian's favored mode of transportation, but this vessel was much stranger. It was beast-like, ferocious. It seemed almost angry just sitting there.

After some preparation of the vehicle, Dr. Whitney briefed Stantish on how to operate it. He was insisting on piloting it for security reasons, as their journey was to take a route through mostly open and unsecured territory. Dr. Whitney maintained that they would be fine, but Stantish wouldn't hear of it. Constant suppressed a smile as he mused that Stantish was perhaps eager at the thought of transitioning his mostly diplomatic role to a practical one. After the lesson was complete, the rest of them climbed into the back and took their seats.

Constant was surprised at how comfortable the carriage was on the inside. The entire interior was coated with a perforated synthetic animal skin, which was to his initial aesthetic displeasingly artificial, but once he settled into his seat, quite pleasurable to the touch. The interior itself was quite dark, almost absent of light—the unlikely black-ness of the materials seemed to dim the light of the entire interior—but as soon as Stantish started the vehicle, it lit up with an impressive and unexpected spectacle of lights, rivaled only by the growling hum of its combustion-based engine.

A light slowly appeared at the other end of the hall: the gate had been raised for them. With a lack of hesitation that allowed little warning to the others, Stantish plunged their vehicle squealing through the bright open aperture, and they quickly disappeared into the desert beyond.

Chapter 5

A long ride through a cold landscape

With some direction from Dr. Whitney, Stantish soon had them en route, northbound on a largely unpopulated section of the North American Highway. As a precaution, the satellite uplink had been disconnected so that their vehicle's activities could not be tracked, forcing them to navigate partly by the vehicle's local sonic and infrared systems, partly by a printed map interpreted by Dr. Whitney, and the rest purely by sight. Before long, they were traveling along a soon empty straightaway, tracing their way through an increasingly impressive and desolate landscape.

Slowly, the scrubby terrain gave way to a shockingly Martian landscape. It was a vast desert basin, sparsely dressed with tall, eroded rock spires. The steel blue sky had given way to massive silver storm clouds that lumbered their way slowly across the ether, emitting a long trail of half-frozen precipitation. The enclosing grayness contradicted the Martian landscape, which was one typically completed with an eternal cobalt blue. Constant was told that this was not naturally the state here, as with many places now on the continent, but a product of an Egolsian accelerated natural disaster, which had caused drastically shifting and severe weather patterns.

The sound of the engine soothed him. The slight warmth of the vessel comforted him. He fell into revery, reflecting on the past day's strange turn of events, and his suspiciousness of the troubling pair of interlopers he had seen in the hallway. He mentioned some of his thoughts on the subject to Dr. Whitney, and she seemed entirely unconcerned, waving it away with her delicate hand. This had been going on for a while, she suggested. She was, rightly so, much more concerned with their present situation, and what their next step was going to be.

The news of the further disintegration of their governing body had not exactly surprised her either. The political and economic situation in their nation had steadily, then quite haphazardly, begun to erode all around her. It was like a cliff on the edge of the sea, she explained. One that ever so slowly and silently starts slipping, rock by rock, into the water. Then almost all a once, sheet by sheet, the whole thing tumbles, rushing and roaring into the spray below. So, while shocking, it was only inevitable.

They were on a timeline here. "This," she said, gesturing to the foreboding clouds looming outside the windows, "is one of our real problems."

A long ride through a cold landscape

"It eroded in much the same way, much like our politics," she continued with a bit of melancholy, "and we just watched it happen. We watched it happen over the course of nearly a century. Little by little, increments of inconvenience gave way to sudden catastrophes that were forgotten as soon as they came, until all at once, the whole system collapsed and our landscape changed forever.

"We can barely farm here now, at least not in most places. And if we cannot farm, we cannot eat. Think of it, this was once one of the most fertile places on our planet, and now it's become a desert with snow storms. Think of that... We have to beg and borrow from our neighbors now, from places that once looked to us for help.

"Many people have found their way roaming out here," she continued, as everyone watched the monotonous landscape roll by. "Others have migrated to other less severe continents, but the cities have become some of the strangest places of all. They all feel like they died and had a new city slapdashed right on top of them. Some parts gleam with the newest, modern high-rises piled right on top of the old ones. In other parts, they have tried to turn buildings into farms, and still, others have been wholly abandoned, and have now been taken over by tribes of feral people.

"In one of these cities, the people walk around the entire day with guns pointed at each other. Can you believe that?" she said turning and leaning toward Constant. "They never stop pointing guns at each other for fear that as soon as they do, someone will kill them. Can you believe it? Another one has forbidden weapons of any kind, but they have also effectively walled themselves in. It's like each of them is trying to find a way to get it right, but none of them are really succeeding. The problem is the whole world as we know it is crumbling, and we don't know what to do."

She sighed and sunk back into her seat, pausing as if she had lost the point, like it had dissipated in the desperation of it all. Finally, she continued, now with the tone of conclusion in her voice.

"This place, the West, is falling apart. And over on the other side of the world is a whole other disaster. There is pretty strong intelligence that one of the countries over there—China to be exact—has been receiving embargoed technology from some visiting species, but we don't know who. Hell, it could even be those same guys you were asking me about." Constant raised an eyebrow, but she just waved her hand and continued.

"But look, we are not interested in politics. We are only interested in one thing—our future as a race, and if we can find a new way of living in all this chaos. That is what they are trying to do at the North Camp, and that is why we are going there." She slumped down in her seat, finally done with her depressing discourse.

"So no, to answer your question," she said, adding with a slow breath, "those beings, whoever they are, do not worry me. What I am most worried about is what we are doing to ourselves."

And now it was her turn to slip away into revery, as they all watched the passing landscape out of the windows, their vehicle still whipping its way down the deserted highway, and the gray clouds passed their reflection over its glassy black surface outside.

A long ride through a cold landscape

* * *

And so they drove on in silence, as the land finally flattened out into vast tracks before them. The light had begun to dim and swallow the long stretching road in a violet-blue glow. The road was almost hypnotic in its monotony. Ahead, Stantish had spotted a dark spec at its vanishing point, growing larger as they hurled down the straight-away towards it. The silence was finally broken by a quiet exchange of words between him and Dr. Whitney.

Stantish seemed concerned by whatever it was, which was not uncommon for his hyper-vigilant state of mind when on an operation, but Dr. Whitney seemed unsettled as well, which in turn unnerved Constant. His time in the field had allowed him to develop a calm perspective in unexpected circumstances, but it had also taught him a certain sensitivity towards the reactions of the locals. That is, if they got scared, he got scared.

The dark object ahead soon revealed itself as a cluster of Egolsian automobiles, stretching across the highway, blocking its path. Stantish brought their vehicle to a stop several lengths in front of it. He held his hand up to indicate to the group to maintain their silence as they intently scanned the obstruction. Owvi, completely oblivious, continued to sleep peacefully in the back.

The blockade appeared to be deserted. Now that they were closer, they could see that it was composed of several cars piled on top of each other, forming a rough line that ran perpendicular to the road. Here and there, patches of metal sheeting had been added in certain places, giving it a fortified appearance. It also, and more to the point, did not appear able to allow passage through, even temporarily. Clearly, it was not a gate, but a fort, and one designed to prevent passage. And it was all too quiet.

That quiet lasted only for a moment, as six figures quickly rose and froze into place from behind the top tier of automobiles. Constant could not see their faces as their heads were wound in cloth, and they appeared to be pointing an array of antique projectile weapons at them.

Stantish sat intensely still, breathlessly sizing the situation.

"What do we do?" Dr. Whitney asked Stantish, deferring to his expertise, clearly unsure of the situation herself.

An unarmed woman appeared from behind the blockade and strode confidently toward their vehicle. She was making a circular motion with one of her hands.

"I think she wants you to roll down your window," Dr. Whitney translated for Stantish. "They might be simply guarding their territory and want us to find another route."

No sooner had she said this than they heard Owvi's voice from the back.

"No, we need to go. NOW." He had suddenly woken up and had not liked what he felt.

Without hesitation, Stantish put the vehicle in reverse and accelerated, the wheels burning on the decayed synthetic floor. The woman lunged at the door as they quickly backed away. He swung the vehicle around and thrust it down the road as fast as it would go.

Constant and Dr. Whitney craned to look behind them through the darkened glass. The woman was retreating back, as two automobiles tore out from behind the fort, kicking up clouds of dust and debris.

"Go. Go! Go!" Dr. Whitney shouted. Stantish immediately throttled the vehicle to its limit, sending it bouncing down the ruined pavement. The two pursuers fell back for a moment, then leapt forward again at a higher acceleration, apparently engaging some modification to their engines.

The roar of the transport's combustion engine was overcome by their pursuer's as they screamed through the dust clouds behind them, their vessels shivering with the unnatural velocity. As the muddy plumes trailed away, their stalkers came into focus. Two figures had protracted themselves from the windows of their automobiles, each aiming firearm at them.

"Stantish!! I think they're going to—" Dr. Whitney began.

Tick tick tick, projectiles smacked the fortified glass at the back of the vehicle, leaving hot white marks on its surface.

"Do we have any weapons?" Stantish shouted at Dr. Whitney. Before she could speak, Constant interrupted.

"No," he said. "I did not come here to hurt anyone."

"We also need to protect Dr. Whitney," retorted Stantish.

"Constant, they are coming," Owvi interjected with an incongruent calm.

The vehicles behind them again shot forward with an almost deranged speed. There was a loud thump, as their pursuers banged into the back of them, sending them momentarily skidding across the road. Stantish swerved off the road, bouncing and sliding into the desert brush. He accelerated. They followed.

One automobile had fallen behind, as the other expertly clung to their tail. The brush around them exploded and burned as they tore a path through it.

Stantish saw on the electric map displayed on the windshield a sharp decrease in elevation ahead of them. He slowed. Dr. Whitney turned to him in response, her eyes enlarged as she intuited his intention.

"It can take it," he replied automatically, catching her expression in his periphery.

Stantish leveled the throttle, taking them directly towards the embankment.

All of a sudden they were weightless. Time slowed for all of them as they flew off the bank. It slowed in that way that one experiences in moments of out-of-body consciousness, and in that moment, Dr. Whitney and Constant turned, looking into each other's eyes as if to say: "Yes, I know. We shall see."

The vehicle bounced violently forward as the technologically advanced shock system strained against the intense impact, shaking their bodies and propelling them forward. The tail end rotated around as they hit the dense earth and slid to the side then back again as Stantish desperately tried to counter their momentum and continue to charge their vehicle forward.

They looked behind them as the forward pursuing automobile followed them off the embankment. It was no sooner in the air than its front end drove into the packed earth like a plow, sending sand and fauna into the atmosphere, digging deeper and deeper till it finally fell backward with a thud, coming to a stop. Steam shot angrily from its crumpled metal front, as the beast sighed in defeat.

Stantish fled on. As he reunited their transport with the

road, the second vehicle quickly appeared in their rear view.

"There is another one," chimed Owvi, without looking.

It was quickly in line behind them. Both sped on, each finding their groove in the chase. Length by length the chaser crept toward them, despite Stantish's best efforts to push the limits of their machine's highest speed.

Suddenly he jammed the breaks, bringing them hopping to a stop, as their pursuer flew past them. Stantish immediately tried to change gears, but the engine suddenly stalled out. Each one of them felt their stomachs sink. The other vehicle was turning around now. They were in big trouble.

Their adversary was now coming straight for them. Stantish ground at the ignition until finally, the engine roared back to life. He slammed on the accelerator, and seemingly to counter logic, headed straight for the other vehicle. They collided.

As Stantish had anticipated, the low sharp front of their transport dug under their attackers' front end, sending it skipping and skidding, trying to break but to no avail. Stantish accelerated and lifted them up and over, sending them rolling off into a cluster of desert brush. He quickly wheeled the car 180 degrees, sliding to a stop facing their former pursuers. Breathing heavily through his nose, he scanned the dusty mist ahead of them, waiting for the attackers to dare to emerge.

The cloud slowly dissipated revealing the crumpled mess of the opposing vehicle. It was bent over a protrusion of rocks hidden amongst a cluster of shrub. It hissed and steamed helplessly, and then finally. A figure slowly crawled out of the twisted window frame of the driver's door and dropped itself unsteadily onto the ground. Stantish put the transport into gear and crept cautiously forward.

As they passed, they saw more clearly the dark figure's form. Shrouded and wound in dusky cloth, their head covering had been torn loose, revealing a surprisingly lithe face. It was a young adolescent girl. She stared at them defiantly from her tan, soot-covered face as they watched her recede. Stantish shifted to a higher gear and they sped on, into the vast expanse of the desert.

* * *

Night came on quickly. The adrenaline was sluggishly waning in their systems. None of them spoke. They wheeled on into the purple night until Dr. Whitney suggested they stop and camp until morning. Stantish and Constant agreed. They had passed the halfway mark and would be able to make it to their destination the following day.

They pulled off the road and drove into a dry gully, out of sight from the highway. They were able to pitch their camp surprisingly quickly, speaking very little, considering their exhaustion. The camping equipment they had brought was modern, and with just a few pulls on some specific cords, it unpacked itself almost instantly into its full set up.

The night air had become crisp and clear, the moon had risen and revealed its fullness. The electric childlike howl of the desert coyotes pierced the quiet of the valley. They sat around a small fire and talked softly as the stars made their way overhead. They had done their best to digest the events of the day and now had left the discussion of the matter to the side in order to contemplate, and more importantly not to fear, the night. Their chills passed as the radiation from the fire warmed their front sides—and their spirits.

Constant, Stantish and Owvi did their best to point out the rough location of their homeworlds to Dr. Whitney in the shivering heavens above. They all remarked how beautiful the view was out here, and how particular their vantage point was of the great rim of their galaxy, as it stretched its way in an iridescent arc across the rolling sky.

* * *

Waking in the morning, Constant noticed immediately that the temperature had dropped. He could see his breath form in plumes right in front of him. The light seemed extra bright outside, shining through the thin walls of the tent, giving everything an eerie glow.

Trying not to wake anyone, Constant unfastened the entrance and slipped out of the tent. He immediately winced at the vivid white light. As his eyes adjusted, they revealed the otherworldly landscape before him. It was white upon white, everything completely covered in a film of softly gleaming snow. It was shockingly beautiful. He had never seen anything like it. It had brought with it a clean, biting cold; a cold that seemed to carry with it an air of death, as if it had gently scoured the life from the endless valleys, and left behind a porcelain casting of its former figure. Constant inhaled and coughed at its pinching temperature.

"They come on quick out here these days," Dr. Whitney

said, coming out of the tent behind him. "No warning."

Constant nodded. The whole valley was dead silent. Whatever small sounds were there were now sucked up by the dampening white blanket that covered everything. There is nothing quite like a desert covered in snow. It was stunningly beautiful, but in all of its pristinely scoured, anti-septic exquisiteness, it simply didn't feel right.

"It's too bad too, that all this moisture won't bring new life to the desert—by this afternoon the sun will have dried it all up. It's like it's teased with this new possibility of life, only to have it burned away, over and over again, like some type of Greek myth." She turned and went back in to help Stantish and Owvi pack up their gear.

Constant had never been on a planet where the weather system was crashing like it was here. He had been places where there were erratic or intense storms, but they were ultimately harmonized with the rest of the surface. Here it was like a ruptured hose, impotently flailing about, spraying itself everywhere, but unable to bring new life to anything.

He assumed the circulation of air and essential heat would eventually find new grooves, apart from the ones that they were apparently being released from, and when that happened, the collective climates would stabilize into an entirely new system. No one knew how or when that would happen, however, or if the surface of the planet would even be inhabitable for humanoids when it did. Some scientists on his planet had even done a very cursory study of the problem before Constant had departed, and had not been able to predict a clear outcome. Nevertheless, it was their conclusion that the Egolsians should abandon trying to rectify the situation, and simply aim their efforts at transitioning to life underground.

In the span of the Galaxy, this was not an uncommon occurrence. In the development of a planet, the surface often becomes too harsh for the indigenous species to exist on it, so they adapt by living life under its surface. Egolsia's two neighboring planets, Mars and Venus, had both gone through this at different times, and their inhabitants had now been living underground for countless millennia.

It was a shame though, for Egolsia to have to confront such an option at such an early stage in its development— and that was without even considering the sheer beauty of its surface. It was in fact known throughout the entire Galaxy for its varied, lush and dramatic landscapes that were quite singular. Very few planets of its small stature were even comparable. And now, because of an imbalance solely of their own making, the Egolsians had accelerated the coming of this inevitability. They were now facing the notion of having to abandon that truly privileged landscape, leaving it to the domain of the flora and fauna of their world, as they huddled under its surface to escape the new brutality of its heat and frost.

* * *

In little time, they packed the transport and aimed it northward. The newly fallen snow seemed to stretch out forever across the gloomily lit landscape. Constant and Owvi watched the pale hills go by, transfixed by their singular beauty, and their endless rolling topology. They seemed to go by so sadly, Constant thought to himself, continuing to reflect on his morning's thoughts, as if they knew the bleakness that was to come for them, and how their few travelers would dwindle in the times to come, until eventually they would be left all alone, in silence.

Stantish and Dr. Whitney had plotted out a new course, carefully selecting rural routes, as none of them wanted a repeat of the previous day's events. Constant could tell Stantish was bothered by them, by his extra focus on his task. Or perhaps he was only projecting—the previous day's unexpected violence had too left him ill at ease. He knew Stantish well enough to know that what he was experiencing was not fear, as he was not easily rattled, but it was more the sting of his pride that was chaffing him. In his mind, as acting security officer, he had allowed them to get into a compromising position, one that might have had disastrous consequences. Stantish was clearly intent on not making that mistake again.

Constant also noticed that his team seemed to be developing an affection for Dr. Whitney. Stantish, in particular, appeared to be displaying an almost fraternal desire to protect her, beyond merely maintaining the safety and security of the mission. Constant too had to admit that she was having an effect on him as well. He kept finding himself absentmindedly watching her as she scanned the horizon. The truth, however, he mused to himself, was that in this strange environment, it was probably to her they should be looking to keep the party safe. Even in this desolate land, it seemed anything could happen, and what did happen here seemed outside of any sort of galactic normality.

Slowly they found the edge of the snow, and the landscape shifted to a staccato array of broad and flat rock formations. It was strikingly vast and austere, a big thundering symphony of stone and space, with huge structures gliding themselves out over the waiting desert floor. It all appeared immovable, eternal, but also as a kinetic moment, like a grand note of music frozen in time.

Dr. Whitney climbed into the back to discuss their arrival plans with Constant. The deep curved seat pushed her toward him, causing sensations of thrill and discomfort to pass unexpectedly through his body. He had, in particular, noticed her scent—it was quite pleasant, like some soothing exotic flower he had never smelled before. He struggled to get comfortable while she began breaking down the rest of their journey, not noticing his fidgeting nor his distraction at all.

She explained they were nearing the semi-permanent encampment that was to be their destination. It was located in the northern part of the middle-west of North America, near a government protected parkland, in a region that until very recently was called the Dakotas. Now it had no name, and because of its harsh weather, was mostly devoid of any inhabitants—they had all either left or succumbed to its new and unexpectedly harsh realities. This, however, had made it a perfect location for the collection of scientists who had gathered there to carry out their activities.

The North Camp, as it was called, was essentially a scientific community populated by a variety of types of people with a range of skills, all oriented to a specific set of goals. To say it was intended to be clandestine would be incorrect, as it was nearly impossible for anything to be a secret nowadays, but it did exist in a delicate balance created by a few behind-the-scenes political ties so that it would be allowed to simply exist unmolested.

She explained further that they would be greeted by the camp leadership upon their arrival, and would most likely be attending an assembly meeting at some point within the following days where they could discuss their options. The assembly was their own form of self-government and helped to set the agendas for the camp. Undoubtedly there would be interest and inquiry by the community on how to best make use of their most valuable guests.

She also warned Owvi to be prepared for some staring, and maybe even frightened or unnerved responses, in their first encounters with the camp's occupants. Most there had not only never seen an extra-terrestrial species before, but some still held the belief that they did not exist at all. So, it could be a shock to be confronted by the reality of his appearance for the first time.

"They will be fine," he said, smiling blithely as he bounced on the spring of the back seat.

"It is you that must make sure they believe we are here in their best interest," Dr. Whitney retorted.

She wrinkled her brow and turned back to Constant. "Anyhow, we will be arriving around nightfall. They should already be expecting us."

Constant again shifted uncomfortably in the seat next to her, their shoulders pressed against each other as they both gazed out opposite windows, watching the receding landscape as they rode silently into the darkening night.

Chapter 6

Destination
North Camp

They switched the engine to a low-hum mode and dimmed the lights to the infrared spectrum, so as to not attract any unwanted attention as they began their near approach to the secure territory in which the North Camp was stationed. Relieved to finally be there, they opened their windows to the fresh night air. Out in the darkened hills beyond, Constant could hear the haunting songs of the invisible bands of Coyotes that sang eerie ballads to each other across the luminescent desert floor. Dusk was spending its last breath glowing red and violet-blue over the low slung mountains that surrounded the valley. The scene stirred in Constant a feeling of deep melancholy, which mixed with the enlivening and mysterious agitation that often accompanied the witnessing of great beauty—it all felt so savage and dangerous and potent with whatever it was that was to come.

As they pulled onto the trail that led up to the encampment, Constant began to make out the flat angular walls that surrounded its south face. It was not completely camouflaged to the degree that if someone were to walk right up to the gate, they would not be able to see that there was a concealed structure standing before them, but to someone speeding by on the highway, or even crossing the plane on foot, it would appear as nearly invisible.

They pulled to a large flat section of wall, where their inconspicuous path came to an abrupt end and shut off the engine. They sat in silence, in the dark, and waited.

Before too long, two dark figures appeared at either window. Dr. Whitney spoke briefly with the guard at her window before he turned around, and made a rotating signal with his hand to some unseen party. The wall was a gate and a gate that was now shivering its way open. Stantish started the engine back up again, and with a few hushed shouts of encouragement, quickly moved the vehicle inside.

* * *

The interior of the compound was much larger than Constant had imagined from the outside. It was sparsely lit, but he could still make out the rough layout of the buildings and grounds as they made their way into the center of the village. Some appeared old and repurposed, and some looked new—it was as if an existing plan that had been laid out in a more organic manner, had then been overlaid with an attempt to create a particular order.

The road swung around, forming a large circle in the

middle of a series of small dome-like buildings. They were directed by the guards to drive up to the center ring, where they stopped and got out. They could see lights speckling the dimly lit center circle, lights which now bobbed and grew brighter as a group of figures walked down the path that bisected it. It all seemed so hushed and tense until a cheerful voice boomed from the approaching group.

"Dr. Zeta, Dr. Whitney, Friends! Welcome." Constant search for the owner of the honey-toned voice.

The figures emerged from the darkness into the lamplight. The voice had come from a very tall, slight-framed, bronze-skinned man, with an impeccable appearance, despite the harshly utilitarian nature of his garb. The voice also did not seem to match the face, until he exposed his broad effusive smile—rows of neat white teeth, seeming to all line up in a gesture of goodwill.

He walked nimbly and confidently toward Constant, grasping his hands. "Dr. Zeta, I'm so glad you decided to come. I'm Frank Larson."

Flanking him were a few other members of the camp, incongruously arranged around him, an eclectic mirror of Constant's own team. The two groups introduced each other, with Owvi standing off to the side smiling quietly remembering Dr. Whitney's words—he did not wish to be a distraction.

A large man with orange swept hair stepped forward as Frank continued his introductions, "...and this is Storm, my security advisor and construction coordinator, and Tii Greene, my chief engineer."

Another figure now stepped forward, in stark contrast to

the intimidating security advisor. She was slight, wisp-like, with generous wide-spread eyes, golden skin, and raven hair that was braided across the top and shorn closely on the sides.

Ignoring the formalities of the introductions, she walked away from the others, over to Owvi in a state of transfixed wonderment. Owvi gazed back with his gentle eyes and extended his hand with a small smile. She took it with a slow tentativeness and smiled.

"Hi," Tii said, introducing herself.

"Tii?" Owvi confirmed her name politely. She nodded.

"Owvi-Alwi-Tovwai." He said, uncharacteristically giving her his full name as she continued to nod. Then added. "I promise I won't read your mind."

"It's OK." She beamed back, still holding his hand. "I don't mind." Then seeming to remember herself, she dropped it and stepped back, and noticing the group had paused for this strange and endearing introduction, made an unsuccessful attempt to collect herself.

Frank broke in.

"Dr. Zeta, new friends, please come. You've all had a long journey here I'm sure. Let us show you your quarters. Storm! Please see that Dr. Zeta's friends here are shown to their rooms. Constant—may I call you Constant?—Come with me and I'll show you to your room personally."

There was a bit of a commotion as his assistants corralled the group, leaving Frank to take Constant's arm and lead him away from the others. Constant looked over his shoulder at Dr. Whitney as they departed, she waved him on with a comforting smile.

Frank led him down an artificially lit street, heading to the North end of the camp. He kept his arm warmly locked in his own as they crunched along the graveled path.

"Dr. Zeta, I can't tell you how happy I am to have you here with us. When I got word you were coming, I was, I was—over the moon!—overjoyed at the opportunity to talk with you. But don't worry there's plenty of time to talk tomorrow, my friend!" he said warmly squeezing Constant's hand, then quickly taking it away as if he got a bit of a shock, "—I'm sure you're quite ready for a rest. I wanted to make sure you were comfortable, so I insisted that you would stay in my quarters. Right up here, just right up here at my house—."

They were walking up to a softly sweeping hill at the northernmost portion of the grounds. They stopped at its base to take in the view. At the top of the gentle ascent was a large faded white dwelling. It had a stately aspect to it, standing tall upon its perch, peering out over its domain, which was now the converted compound's grounds. It gave an odd impression—as if its darkened windows expected to see a much different vista before it. It must have been the original principal dwelling of the estate, Constant mused. It was aged and kept from disrepair with an apparent economic effort, but it still commanded the hillside with quiet dignity.

A small deteriorating wooden box, sitting atop a pedestal near to where he stood, caught Constant's eye. Affixed to the side of it was a curious ragged metal banner. He reached out and placed his hand delicately on it; he felt something. The base of his skull shuddered mildly as a new tableau flashed before his mind's eye.

He saw a whole scene emerge before him, slowed down in the unfolding of time and illuminated by a vivid sunlight. There was a young Egolsian girl dressed in a bright white smock tumbling down the lush green hill, giggling as she went. He saw the child's mother opening the front door, scolding her with a wagging finger. He saw a man on the edge of the field motioning to other figures toiling within it. It was an exquisite scene, heart-wrenching and almost melancholy in its sheer beauty. There was happiness in the air, a feeling that the day would last forever…

Waking from his reverie, Constant felt Frank's hand gently shaking his shoulder.

"Dr. Zeta? Dr. Zeta?" Frank had noticed that he had ceased responding to him, and was now transfixed by the sight of the house.

"It once was another kind of home. In a much different time." Constant finally replied softly, the scene before him now fading into the reality of the present.

Frank at first paused, then answered, now himself staring at the house "Yes, yes it was," he said shaking his head. "It was a time that never really existed," he finished cryptically. "Come, let's go in, it's getting late. We will have plenty of time to speak about all of this when I show you the grounds tomorrow."

Frank showed him inside, then departed for his own temporary quarters. Constant made an attempt to retire and secure himself some well needed rest, but he was unable to sleep. He was haunted by the vision of the old house on the hill, and the artifice of the new encampment affixed to its feet. He contemplated both these two worlds, laid atop of each other, and how both of their fates now hung in the balance. He did not get much sleep that night.

Chapter 7

Intentions laid bare

Constant rose with the sun the next morning and found Frank already awake, nearly bouncing at his door. There was much to do that day, and he wanted to make sure he had enough time to personally show Constant around. He assured Constant that his colleagues were being well taken care of and they set off on their tour.

It was a cool, crisp morning, a soft luminescent mist hung about the camp, lighting it almost without shadow. As they strolled down the hill from the house, the compound unfolded itself before them. It was composed of an eclectic group of buildings, varying in age, architecture, and era. The original estate had been a farm, that radiated out from the house on the hill, flanked by a grove of trees and sprawling cultivated patches of terra.

The entirety of the front half had been rearranged and overlaid with the more recent encampment. It was partially composed of ad-hoc structures that looked like they had been built from recovered materials—sheds, small dwellings, and longhouses, which hinted at different purposes—and the rest were obviously much newer and modern structures that were laid out in a way that seemed to attempt to recover order to the plaza. Many of them were bright white and geometric, all oriented around the center circle that Constant and his team had passed through the night before. A large white geodesic dome sat as a singular centerpiece amongst a series of low box-like structures and an array of tall narrow antennas.

On the opposite side towards the fields sat what appeared to be a small stable. It was curiously similar to the kind that housed certain quadrupeds used for husbandry in the rural districts of Constant's homeworld. Its presence gave him a bit of excitement, as he always found it particularly interesting to observe the similarities and differences between the animals of different planets, and marvel at the way the small diversities were almost always the most compelling.

They walked through the center of the compound towards the front of the grounds with Frank warmly holding Constant's arm. He explained to him the fortification of the front wall and how its main use was to preserve a low profile for the encampment. It kept it mostly hidden from travelers crossing the plain, which happened from time to time. The region was particularly unpopulated, which was one of the factors that had influenced their choice for the location of the community, as the risk of attack or harassment, or even mistaken discovery by a passing traveler, was low. The very few people who did populate the surrounding range kept mostly to themselves, but enough members of the collective knew the fortification's value, and that it could not be risked. So when Storm, the community's appointed security officer, had proposed it be built, they did not spare on the details.

As he had observed on his approach, the wall was nearly invisible from the wide plain, which they reverently referred to as the "Grand Mile," and which composed the camp's southern border. Only a studying eye might be able to make out an angle or two that was disharmonious with nature. Even as one approached, it was hard to see, almost until you were right upon it when you would start to recognize the seldom used path to the gate or see the slight horizontal window slits cut into the rock.

As Frank lead Constant through a doorway into a tall narrow corridor, he explained that the wall was composed mainly of a thick structure of rocks, piled together with strategically placed plants and painted netting, behind which was the winding hallway they were now walking down. The primary function of this chamber was to allow access to the narrow horizontal slits they had cut into the wall that allowed them to observe anyone approaching undetected.

Secondarily, the internal chamber could be used as a defensive bunker against raiders, because of its position and formability, and also act as a shelter in case of extreme weather. Although they did have a smaller series of interconnected underground chambers under the camp more suited for that, there had been occasions where they had used it for just that purpose.

They exited the wall out of its northeast door, which placed them around the back of the central geodesic dome and its surrounding buildings. Frank explained that they collectively functioned as the technology center—the "nervous system" as he put it—of their compound.

This nervous system was mostly focused on blocking satellite detection from the observational craft that orbited Egolsia, Frank explained, so as to allow them to work and communicate unwatched and unmolested. The larger of the antennas let them transmit directly with a small handful of locations under a secure channel. The rest were tasked solely with scrambling invasive imaging and blocking auditory detection. It was more than likely, he continued, that the North American military had images of their compound, but they had at least been able to get it not-so-officially marked as a non-threatening scientific research center. This was due solely to the tireless and tactful efforts of Dr. Whitney and Ambassador Able to secure the much needed designation. Unfortunately, they lived in a time when anything undocumented by the government was considered a threat, and so they spent a lot of energy trying to minimize any attention.

The special classification that allowed for this level of autonomy for their work was labeled as "Scientific Research of the Sustainable Means of Agricultural Production and Food Processing." This was, in truth he explained, their central aim, though the underpinnings of what they were studying touched on some very sensitive and volatile topics. Namely, naturally constructed energy sources and the reverse modification of organic compounds, which was something that was very closely monitored by the government, particularly for the economic interests they represented.

Intentions laid bare

Frank explained all this as he led him through the corridor that bisected the central control center. As they made their way, they passed a series of small rooms sparsely populated with large electronic machines, humming and fluttering away at some indecipherable purpose. Constant was not himself technically inclined but mused that Owvi would love to spend some time pouring over the seemingly arcane systems.

The corridor eventually led them into the interior of the dome structure, which opened out into a large bright spherical space, strutted with geometrically spun walls glowing with soft iridescent light. Within it contained tiers upon tiers of plant life and several levels of equipment, sprawling and patchwork, that seemed to expand out from a curved central console. Two Egolsian engineers stood before it, lost in their work, attending to the ever blinking lights that speckled the cracked and taped panels. They did not look up until Frank and Constant were right on top of them, and gave a start as Frank began to introduce one of them as their chief technician—Hayward.

Hayward turned and rose with an air of irritation. His face was narrow and drawn and mostly swallowed by a tangled but plush beard. All that escaped it was a thin pointed nose, and a pair of round dark spectacles. Constant noticed his unease as Hayward pinched his forehead, waiting for whatever inconvenient question that Frank was going to ask him. It ended up being a request to elucidate Constant on what exactly it was that they did there. Hayward exhaled and answered with a rapid, mercurial exposition, rubbing his forehead and gesticulating wildly to the piles of invisible examples arranged in the air around them.

"Well besides spending a great deal of time monitoring modulations for deep packet inspection probes, analyzing any light-wave slash micro-wave slash infrared wave frequencies for any potential systematic surveillance patterns—basically listening if anyone is listening to us—we spend the rest of the time monitoring local radio transmissions simply as a precaution against possible raiders, hackers and any other unwanted curious guests you see. But mostly after that we watch the weather and try to track or anticipate flash storms, which of course are happening more and more these days… and where did you say you where from?" Hayward suddenly asked sharply.

Constant smiled, "I didn't."

"You look like you're from Norway," he continued, appearing not to notice his answer.

"That has been told to me. No, I do not come from there, I am in fact from the Artioovian-Cal—"

"You sure you're not from Noway? You sure look it…," he again replied, pinching his forehead, while seemingly trying to decipher Constant's authenticity with the power of his eyes.

Constant maintained a cordial smile but did not reply. Frank took him by the arm and led him away, remarking at their unease.

"It's not you, I assure you," Frank replied with a smile, as they exited the dome, leaving Hayward to immediately return to obsessing over his suspicious kingdom.

"They have to spend an unfortunate amount of time monitoring that system, as there are few here that can do it," Frank continued. "Their job makes them naturally suspicious of anyone, spending so much time evaluating whether or not anything they pick up is a threat to us or not."

"How often does that occur?" asked Constant.

Frank paused. "Not often. Usually, it's the weather we worry about these days. It's been growing more erratic, and more destructive in the past couple of years. Up until then, it was less so in this part of the country... anyway, we did have a few incidents with outsiders in the beginning, but not for a while now, knock wood."

"Knock wood?" Constant paused, asking him with genuine curiosity.

"Oh yes, sorry. An idiom. It means good luck," Frank replied, laughing off the tension of the previous topic.

Of course nearly every culture Constant had come into contact with held some conception of this idea of luck, but for the Egolsians, Constant gleamed, it carried more colorful attachments and varied meanings than any others he knew of. Case in point was the pensive, almost religious, tone in which Frank had just wielded it. All of these cultures too carried their share of accident, unpredictability, and chaos—from the most evolved to the most primitive—and they all seemed to have their own particular relationship to it. It often manifested as a certain impalpable, existential outlook on such events, especially the disastrous and misfortunate kind. For the Egolsians however, they seemed the most plagued by this phenomena and seemed to only have such a shifting and insufficient understanding of it, that they knew not how to digest such moments or find any way to prevent them.

Constant nodded in sympathy. "You are still afraid of them," he said, stopping to turn to Frank.

Frank looked back at him. "Yes. Like I said, we've had a couple of incidents," he replied with a tone as if he were confessing to something he did not like to talk about. He took his arm and began leading him down another corridor.

"Come, this way," Frank reluctantly continued. "Back in the early days, before we had the wall, and before Storm joined us, we lived here in more like an improvised commune. Things were a little chaotic then, a little unclear you see, though, about what we were trying to do—that doesn't say much for now I know—but if we had a passerby that needed help, we'd give it to them. This was really before there were any raiders or bandits, or at least any that we'd heard of, and so we took everyone at their word. What else were we to do?

"So, on one particular evening, two strangers arrived at our camp. It was a man and a woman, both sad and dirty from the road. They were soft-spoken and scrawny, and just asked for some food, and to lay by the fire for the night, and they would be on their way in the morning. They seemed harmless, and at that time we had plenty of food, so we fed them and let them stay the night.

"Come morning, the man had gone. His female companion had made some excuse, saying he must have wandered off somewhere. Not long into the day though, someone spots about a dozen people moving real quick across the Grand Mile. We asked the woman if she knew them, and she said she didn't know anything about it. They were traveling across the plain real fast, but as soon as someone was able to make them out, they saw that they were carrying what looked like weapons and shouted out an alarm to the rest of us. But by then it was too late, and right at that same moment, this woman—the one who we had fed and let stay the night—pulls a knife out of her sleeve, grabs one of the female engineers next to her, and puts the blade to her throat.

"They came in pretty quick after that, with us all just standing here. They stole most of our supplies, and then they just left, about as quick as they came—they seemed just about as scared of us as we were of them. And it wouldn't have been that bad if that was the end of it—they didn't really take that much, and no one really got hurt that bad."

Frank paused, shaking his head, remembering. "The problem was though, that they did come back, a few times more even, and some people did get hurt—bad. We weren't sure if we were going to be able to stay. But after Storm got here, we built the wall, and he finally chased them away—for good."

"How did he do that?" asked Constant.

Frank paused. "He killed some of them."

* * *

As they exited the complex, Frank knew partly by the cool air around him that Constant was not pleased, but mainly he knew because Constant had told him quite squarely so as they stepped out onto the gravel path.

"You cannot achieve an equitable end through the use

of violence," Constant challenged him. "It will only eventually produce more violence. I would have thought your people would have understood this by now, at least at a fundamental level—after so much time, so much experience with this. So many of your ostensibly noble goals you attempt to protect, or further, are all eventually subverted by violence, often resulting even in many of your greatest creations being destroyed. And why?" Constant asked him with genuine interest.

"We know Dr. Zeta. I mean I think we know, or maybe we don't. Maybe we forget. But still, you do not fully understand this world yourself. Often we have no choice," Frank argued, but even to him, his words felt well worn and thin.

"Forced to commit violence on each other? In war? To protect what?" Constant retorted. "In the defense of the destruction of your own body, perhaps, but in how many occurrences is that the exact case? When you destroy the beings of your kind or any beings outside the reciprocal flow of eating and being eaten required by nature, you subvert the role of your own God. You seek to judge the value of life, your interests over the value of your opposer's. How is it you believe you possess this ability? Do not your very own religions instruct you that this is not the reality of the situation?" Constant was not letting up. Frank felt his full intention.

"I understand Constant, trust me I do," Frank responded with a sigh. "These are conditions that we live under here—a constant choice between a bad option and a worse one. But we're trying Constant, I promise you, we're trying to do better. We've got one foot in the old world, and one foot in the new one, and we're trying to take only the essentials—only the good ones—into that new world. That is what this place represents to us. That's why we decided to protect it so fiercely, why we believe we can make that decision. Otherwise, what else are we supposed to do? Simply lay down and die?" Frank shrugged, stopping now to look at Constant. "All I ask is that you keep an open mind—please, just don't condemn us yet. Just let me show you what we're doing here. Please, let me show you—"

Constant acquiesced and let Frank lead him off to a series of low gray buildings, tucked in the shadow of the dome. They entered an adjacent synthetic stone vault through a sliding metal panel. It took a few moments for their eyes to adjust before what appeared to be two huge combustion engines emerged from the gray-blue interior.

"These, Dr. Zeta, are just one of the necessary attachments of our old world," Frank said, placing his hand on one of their grease dusted hulls. "Probably one of the biggest inventions of the previous centuries—and probably one of the central reasons of our current undoing. But we have to have it here. We don't want to use it, but we keep it still to supplement our power, simply because all the other sources we have, our current conditions prevent us from making full use of them."

Frank went on to describe how they were originally fossil fuel generators but had been converted to a hybrid biofuel, and explained that when needed, they could temporarily power the entire control center. Primarily they powered the electronics of the control center with a system that essentially intercepted sunlight, and fed its energy into hydro-based batteries. As far as were contemporary standards on energy, this was considered a good system. However, Frank articulated, from the collective's point of view, it had some fundamental drawbacks. Primarily it was the fact that atmospheric disturbances, such as inclement weather, or the diminished amount of daylight—such as during their winter months, greatly to mildly reduced its output, rendering it ultimately undependable.

The battery systems did allow the storage of electricity when there was less input, but the overall load of the command center often demanded more than the sunlight interceptor system could maintain. And so, because they viewed the monitoring and blocking systems as more or less essential to their project, they had installed the combustion generators and used them on an intermittent basis. They had designed them to run off a fuel created from some of the crops they were developing there.

They knew however that this system was not going to be right in the long term, and eventually, they would have to move on from it, because parts were just no longer accessible or re-creatable. And moreover, the increasing demands of their experiments were quickly outpacing its capacity, and so, they had included into their aim here the pursuit of finding new means of generating the energy that they so desperately needed. This aim was now becoming more and more central to all the work at the North Camp.

"Constant—I must confess—this is one of the reasons I was so excited about meeting you and having you come here…" Frank stopped, looking him in the eye. "I want—I wanted to ask you if you would show us another way…"

Frank paused, looking at Constant expectedly.

"Yes, well, that is why I—" Constant replied.

"I want you to show us clean fusion," Frank interjected.

There it was. Frank had finally laid bare his intention. Constant, for his part, was not able to suppress his smile. Frank's face seemed to fall in inverse proportion, already anticipating the refusal.

"Mr. Larson," he began, gently returning to his formalities. "I truly wish to help in any way that is possible. But that point, in particular, is not possible. I'm afraid there is a very strict embargo against your planet."

"Yes, yes, I know of the embargo," Frank looked down, grimacing. "It's just…"

He paused for a moment, drifting in his thoughts, before looking back up again with his warm smile. "Let's keep walking. Perhaps, we can return to the subject again later…"

Constant nodded politely as if to say the answer would be the same. But Frank was unflappable and took his arm once again.

"Come, let me show you what it is that we actually make here—I'll think you'll find it of interest!" Frank said, excited again as if his somber thoughts were now long in the past.

They briskly walked out, arm in arm, off to explore the purpose of this quite singular—Constant thought to himself—and unusually hopeful, group of people.

* * *

Frank led him to a very large, low, glass topped building. Inside, it had the same clear and warm glow of light as the dome, which cast itself softly over its symmetrical repetitious geometric interior. Its contents were primarily an abundance of a surprisingly, under the circumstances, lush green moss that nearly covered the entire volume of the space.

The interior itself was divided into banks upon banks of water tables. Frank strode out amongst them in front of him. "This is the modified moss we use to make what we call 'Pema,'" he gestured out proudly over the banks, both arms outstretched. "This is our central focus of study here—and also one of our primary forms of nutrition here at the camp."

He motioned for Constant to join him over by one of the water tables. He plucked a small fragment and rubbed it between his fingers, showing its bright green pulp to Constant, before unselfconsciously sucking it from his finger with reverence.

"We are able to distill this down and make a highly nutritious concentrate. It can be consumed fresh, and a dried version of it can last years, even in space." He paused in apparent reverie, wondering at the sight of the life-giving plant. It was a vision that he had no doubt seen so many times, but one that he also evidently regarded as a sort of mana. Remembering himself, he shook himself from his fascination and once again addressed Constant.

"You see Dr. Zeta, as I assume you are aware, we may be heading for another big disaster. All this new weather has been more than just an annoyance to us, more than just an impediment to our ability to create the energy we need—it's keeping us from being able to grow enough food to feed everyone. The weather has all but destroyed modern agriculture on this continent. The topsoil is disintegrating and blowing away. Places that were once fertile are becoming deserts. There are still pockets where we can grow, but it is not nearly enough—it is becoming more and more impossible to grow our own food, to sustain our people. And that means we are at the mercy of the few countries where this is not a problem yet. This is all compounded by the fact that trading and importing have become more difficult due to this recent destabilization. And what the land can actually provide goes almost exclusively to the few people that can afford it. But not for long. In some places, all the people are starting to starve; the rich as well as the poor. Fifty years ago, this was the most abundant country in the world, now we don't know how we're going to last until tomorrow. Things are deteriorating fast.

"We know many methods of terraforming, but the areas are too big and water too precious. That's why we are here inventing not only agricultural methods, but the plants themselves that can withstand these conditions—ones that can grow underground, in the course soil, with minimal greenery aboveground. So far we have not been able to completely solve this, so we've switched focus to the production of Pema."

Constant walked over to one of the water tables and began studying the bright green carpet that covered it with a focused curiosity.

Frank continued. "Pema has been quite a savior for us, and some forms of it have already been employed in some of our impoverished areas. It is highly nutritious, dried so you can store it, light so you can move it, and you can sustain yourself on only a few grams of it a day. I would have to admit that it's not a very pleasant substitute for a real meal, but, you know—the times have changed."

He paused, staring off into the precious confines of the brightly lit room.

"The problem is just the power it takes to create it…," he added slowly, with a sideways glance at Constant. Constant caught the expression but didn't reply directly. He was still regarding the greenery with an intent gaze as if trying to decipher its molecular make-up with his naked eye.

"Yes, I have seen something like this before," he replied standing up straight, smoothing his jumpsuit. "There are a few species that I've met who spend generations in interstellar travel, and so rely heavily on food like this for their expeditions," he added, now turning to Frank with a meaningful eye.

"Yes, well we did get help with the idea," Frank replied with a cryptic smile. "Anyhow, like I said, the power we need to create is an unfortunate burden on our energy supplies, and keeps us well tied to the past..."

Constant looked at him blankly. Frank shrugged his shoulders and gestured towards the door.

"Come. Let's walk."

* * *

As they exited the processing center, they noticed Owvi and Tii approaching from another side of the water banks. They were blissfully unaware of Frank and Constant's presence, walking with their faces beaming towards each other. As they approached, Tii laughed and seemed to respond to something Owvi hadn't apparently vocalized.

"Owvi!" Constant called out to him. "I see you're making friends—" he smiled, then lightly scolded, "I hope you haven't forgotten your agreement," he said referring to the diplomatic suspension of telepathy that they had agreed to while on Egolsia.

"It's OK, Dr. Zeta. I don't mind it—it's quite amazing in fact." Tii immediately defended him, grasping where Constant was going with this. "He's going to teach me how to do it," she countered with a blithe smile.

"Well, I suppose the restriction is there for your comfort after all, so if you indeed do not mind it—" Constant replied with a wave of his hand. He knew these restrictions were mainly just a show for the easily ruffled Egolsians.

"No, not at all. Owvi told me about the restriction," she interrupted. "I guess it makes sense when you consider the temperament of some of my people. They can be suspicious and fearful of what they at first do not understand." The smile faded a bit on her face.

"Yes well, it can be difficult to trust someone when you believe they can enter your mind without your permission—and you yourself are unable to do the same. So I do see their point of view," Owvi broke in.

"Well," her smile returned as she turned her gaze to Owvi. "I trust Owvi, and he has promised to show me how, so soon it will not be so one-sided."

Owvi nodded, suppressing his own smile.

"He's also already shown me some concepts that might

help with the Pema production," she beamed turning to face Frank.

A bell rang cheerfully in the distance as if in punctuation, interrupting them all—it was the time of day for them to sit and eat. And with that, they all left to sup together.

Chapter 8

New faces

The structure in which they partook their mid-day meal was not much more than a grand tent. For its primitive construction, it was lifted in the center to a quite high elevation. Though essentially made of cloth and sticks, the exaggerated concave shape gave it a reverent and ceremonious feel, and indeed the structure was built for this sacred purpose; the taking in of life-giving food.

There was a cheerful hum under the lazily flapping roof, and a breeze passed through its fine net walls. Constant found the atmosphere quite uplifting. He was also quite happy to see all the faces he had not been able to see the night before. In fact, this was the most Egolsians he had ever seen all at once, with his own eyes.

He was particularly stuck with the wide variation of their faces and body types. With all of the common stories and intrigue surrounding them as a people, this was a fact about them that was often under discussed, though its unfortunate superficial bi-product was conspicuously at the center of all of their problems; their outer differences. It was one of the things that Constant found quite intriguing about the Egolsians, and he was eager to now observe them together in their diversity firsthand.

In the realm of their mannerisms, say the table manners he was now witnessing, they were all fairly similar, but in their vibrations and physical expressions, shapes and sizes, they were all quite different. He could see the true blessing of all this variety, but he was also acquainted with its curse. Most planetary-centric species with noticeable regionally specific physical differences had evolved past this variety and, over the course of eons, blended together into one. That said, in many places this homogenization had not necessarily extended to tribal and regional customs and cultures. Nor did it include individualism. In fact, the two were often found in inverse proportion to each other, in some universal biological irony: the more they looked the same, the more they tended to pursue their own individuality, and the more they looked different, the more they seemed content to be the same. It was, unwittingly for them, a somewhat embarrassing illusion that the Egolsians still held fast to—that they were all so very different.

It was more common for differences to be found throughout a solar system itself, both as it portends to a particular species varying from planet to planet, and extra-special; finding a slight to wide variety of species across the planets. Constant's world, in fact, was one of the former.

So it was very unusual for a single race to be so varied and colorful on a single planet. It indeed was remarkable, as each meaningful aspect of the species was articulated in a visible spectrum of differing shapes and sizes, each manifesting in their own way in the construction of their planetary bodies. It was as if their own physiology and psychology had been explicitly laid out in a beautiful band of tones and hues, expressing all of the nuances of the human anatomy and experience that could be found within each individual. From this point of view, Egolsia truly was a beautiful and colorful world.

The curse of this came only later when—for whatever reason, though no doubt helped by the Egolsian's predisposition to judge everything based solely on surface appearance—they began to believe they were all, in fact, different races, and not all from the same origin and members of the same great family. This was unfortunately exacerbated by their power possessors, who found they could manipulate their people by fanning false feelings of superiority and enmity, in order to allow their planetary brethren to be robbed, raped, and enslaved while the rest of them stood passively by.

Even though it was illogical, even though they all knew and accepted that they came from one single mother—a notion uncharacteristically supported by both their science and their religion, and perhaps one of the only things they did agree on—they had become convinced that they were, in fact, separate races, and forgot that they were all, in truth, actual brothers and sisters.

This strange blindness was further typified by the fact that they were also quite unable to distinguish some of their galactic or even solar neighbors from themselves. In other words, the Egolsians believed all of their brothers and sisters to be from different races, yet when confronted by a being from an entirely other human race, from an entirely different planet, they believed them to be one and the same, simply because the complexions of their planetary bodies matched. Because of this, their cousins on the second planet from their sun, known on Egolsia as Venus, had been, until very recently, able to freely move about their modern world on diplomatic missions, until it was noticed their aging process proceeded at a much slower rate.

All of this filled Constant's mind as he looked around the room at their carefully averted eyes; he was barely able to suppress his amusement at the camp members' attempts not to crane their necks to look at him. He caught one of them stealing a glance at Owvi, who himself was engrossed in conversation with Tii. Stantish, as he sat with Storm, for his part they all but ignored. He perceived this discreet effort to appear nonchalant as a sort of politeness on their part, so as not to make their guests uncomfortable. They obviously saw their ability to handle Constant and his team's presence as a mark of being evolved and broad-minded individuals.

It did not take an evolved perception, however, to tell that they were brimming with anticipation to finally and formally meet them. Constant shared the feeling. He had been told that there would be a community meeting that night at which he would be introduced to all of them, and they would have a chance to converse and ask him questions about his mission here. Needless to say, Constant too was counted amongst the eager ones for this to finally transpire. For him—and for them—this was a moment of Contact.

New faces

* * *

As their meal time came to an end, Frank excused himself from Constant, leaving him to his own devices for the rest of the afternoon. Constant welcomed the opportunity and decided to use the time to stroll about the grounds. He had been looking forward to the chance to spend some time exploring at his ease.

Crossing the town's center circle, he headed straight for the stables. He was eager to see with his own eyes the form in which the animals of husbandry took on this planet. He had seen some images of them in his studies of course, though he had mostly occupied himself with geographical and political briefs, and synopses of modern cultural shifts.

What he did read about the Egolsian's relationship with the animals of their planet was that it had eventually become relegated to them now being kept primarily as what they called "pets" and of only a few types. All other relationships, even the most scientific—with the exception of those conducted solely at a healthy distance—had become considered abusive. It was a warranted overreaction, as in the time preceding this shift in attitude, the Egolsians, through their reckless behavior, had permanently destroyed over half of the species on their planet.

It was also noted that many of their chosen types of pets had become integrated into life at nearly the same level as other Egolsians, and had begun to adopt many of their particular behaviors, such as dressing in their fashion, and even joining them in polite practices such as eating at their public tables, without their keepers.

Currently, though, this had shifted back towards their more primal traditions simply out of necessity. Previously husbandry had been practiced outside of modern life and the daily going-ons of society, so much so that it had been almost completely replaced by robotic apparatus, and had all but disappeared. In recent years, however, based on the breakdown of the trade systems and energy sources that Frank had explained to him, localized farming practices had reemerged into the view of daily life, even in the most urbanized cities.

As he entered the stable, Constant's nose winced as he was immediately hit with the strong and familiar smell that accompanied such structures all across the universe. Worlds apart, it still smelled the same: sweetly sour and overwhelmingly pungent. He marveled at the pang it had created—the smell of the dung had made him involuntarily long for his home.

Towards the back he recognized the shape of Dr. Whitney, standing next to a broad quadruped, absorbed in the brushing of its dark black coat, silhouetted against the far open door. Constant paused. The scene had given him another involuntary feeling: Dr. Whitney, standing now as a woman before him, was truly beautiful. There was a certain grace in the sureness of her movements. And in her unspoken but palpably affectionate connection to the great quadruped before her, he experienced a glimmer of that organic love that binds all living things together.

He moved towards them quietly, with the intention of silence, so he could bring the lovely beast further into focus without disturbing it. It bore a shining bluish black coat and had lean and powerful muscles. Its spirit seemed so buoyant that it almost leapt from its body—it was like a giant heart muscle that had sprouted legs, ready to spring and float over the countryside. Constant marveled at it, and could not help his reverie.

The scene of the two standing there had turned his mind back again to memories of home. His home planet had a quadruped very similar to what he assumed was the Egolsian "Horse." On his tribal land, they had a relationship with an animal called the "Fjorjoovan" or "Fors"— whose appearance was a quite close cousin, however with a few striking differences.

The first difference was the possession of horns. Their horns were not composed of bone or keratin, as was universally common with quadrupeds supplied with horns or antlers, but structured out of a matted type of fibrous hair. They twisted and turned, at basis following the similarly universal fractal pattern of most antlers, yet were swept back, and grew wildly and unpredictably on their second or third level, whether minimally or prolifically, to create a pattern as personal as the human fingerprint. They looked like tall, protruding nerves more than anything else.

There was much debate on his planet as to whether or not the Fors had evolved these horns specifically for mating, for purposes of fashion, or whether it was some other much deeper and profound symbol that only nature could answer. Also uncommonly, both sexes possessed them, yet neither used them in any sort of violent contests of dominance, as was common with horns and antlers of certain other beasts. Nor was there any status connected to their shape or elaborate nature, apart from their subjective aesthetic appeal. Either way, it made them almost impossible to capture against their will, and moreover, it made each one of them quite individually beautiful.

The second attribute that set the Fors apart from the Egolsian horse was their coloration. They shared some similarities, as both black and white varieties could be found, but their most common color was red. It was the same noble color as the desert terrains where they evolved, which were overly rich in iron, and shone brightly in red on red striations.

Seeing Dr. Whitney brushing the steed brought back the electricity of nostalgia for his home planet, and he instinctively paused to collect himself. Dr. Whitney noticed him lurking and looked up.

"Dr. Zeta! How are you finding yourself on this beautiful day?" she said, her smile lighting up the dimly sunlit stable. "Come meet my friend, Captain," she said to the animal cheerfully. "You're not afraid of horses are you?" she asked, turning back to Constant.

Constant smiled and matter-of-factly replied. "No, of course not."

He began stroking the coat and speaking with the same quiet, matter-of-fact tone, introducing himself to the magnificent beast. It brayed and cocked its head as if in response.

Constant smiled. "It reminds me of home."

Dr. Whitney paused her careful brushing. "Really? You have horses on your planet?"

"A kind. We call them 'Fors.' We have had a long lasting

relationship with them for many millions of years—since before our recorded history. Much like yourselves," he replied with a hint of pride.

"That's fascinating. I wouldn't have thought..." Dr. Whitney seemed struck into wonderment by this detail.

"Yes, inter-species relationships are quite common in many of the planets I have visited. It is part of the harmony of organic life. Those who no longer have them have all constructed artifice in their place. I can't say those are the most pleasant places I've been. There are many relationships you Egolsians have to other species here that do not recommend you well to the rest of the civilized galaxy, but this does not appear to be one of them," he said, stroking the horse's chin.

Dr. Whitney paused in reflection. "I hope you're right about us," she added without looking up.

"So do I," Constant replied. "So do I."

Chapter 9

New friends

After Dr. Whitney finished with her grooming—aided by Dr. Zeta's surprisingly skillful help—she invited him to accompany her on a late afternoon ride. It would afford her a chance to spend some time with this truly otherworldly mind—one she was now growing not only more intrigued by, but also fond of. She offered to show him the fields and the terrain beyond the camp, something Constant had already expressed an eagerness to see.

They embarked on their trek out of the West gate. She could not help being impressed by the ease at which he rode, occasionally speaking softly in his horse's ear. She was fascinated by him. The impression she had gotten from him was mixed. Although she was one part of the driving force behind getting him here to North Camp, she had a natural reservation, almost a suspicion, of the arguably few visitors to her planet that she had actually met.

She no doubt recognized these visitors' evolved attributes, and very often their overtly intellectual, moral and technological superiority. She fully believed that their advanced minds and learning—especially their comparably vast experience in evolving through their own societal dilemmas—could greatly aid the people of her planet in finding a new way of living. All this might have been true, but the thing she found hard to believe was the notion that they could truly understand the problems they faced here on Earth.

In her few interactions with otherworldly beings, she had gotten the definite sense that they could not comprehend why the beings of her planet could simply not "do" or "not do" so many things that to them seemed rational or morally self-evident. And honestly, she had to admit that if she herself had not arisen on this planet, it would be difficult for her to understand why they did so many things that, when held up to the light of reason, just seemed crazy.

And so, as far as Constant went, he had immediately fulfilled upon her expectations of acute perceptiveness with the same accompanying intellectual aloofness—but he had begun to grow on her. Maybe he would prove to be different after all, she thought to herself. Seeing him now, with great ease finding his way along this foreign trail, upon a horse he'd never met before, filled her with a tenderness and sympathy for him. It gave her hope.

They crossed over the hillside to the octagonal patchwork of fields where the camp grew most of their food. Despite a highly orchestrated effort, only about half the sections were green, the others were brown or barren. Some were unsuccessful experiments in hybrids they were developing, others were traditional staples that they were just unable to grow due to the conditions of the soil and lack of rain. This was the original focus of the grand experiment here: the production of simple agriculture in the poisoned and arid soil, in a rapidly shifting environment. And the simple conclusion so far was thus: they couldn't do it. This was why they were now focusing more and more on Pema. Dr. Whitney marked a struggling patch of soil to Constant as they passed.

Their study had been two-fold, she explained. First off, they had sought to create several hybrid root vegetables, ones that could live successfully in the hot, dry acrid earth, with minimal need for water. The second area of study was to find means of natural irrigation and plant rotation to rehabilitate the scorched earth with minimal input.

Both approaches were based on the central philosophy which pervaded everything that they studied at the camp: whatever methods and means they discovered or labored to create must number one, require little import and cause near zero impact on the surrounding environment; number two, need only the most economical of efforts to produce and maintain; number three, be master-able by the common citizen; and number four, be repeatable as near to ad-infinitum as possible. They applied these rules to not only agriculture but to manufacturing, energy generation and consumption. It was their belief that for their society to have any possibility of moving forward without first a total collapse, they must somehow master these precepts.

She further explained that in the pursuit of these ideals, however, they did not wish their future to suffer from some sort of technological amnesia. Nor was it even a practical option for them at that time. The problem was up until that point, commercial progress had been given exclusive credit for the advancement of technology, but a number of Egolsians now rejected that idea. The inventor did indeed need the benefactor, but solely for the development of an invention, not for its inspiration. And then that benefactor could take many forms—it need not be a corporation or a commercial market, but an entity that simply needed to provide the means and force, which could even come in the form of a vote.

The answer they were searching for was then not a method that would allow them to eliminate technology entirely from their lives, but a way for them to shrink it down and have it fit more reasonably in their world; for it to serve them, and not for it to be the master of them. They did not want to, as the saying goes, throw the baby out with the bath water—

"The what?" Constant broke in.

"The bath water—it's an idiom, an expression."

"You do that here too?"

"No, it's just an expression…"

"A very strange one," Constant remarked, looking out of the side of his eyes.

"Yes—look Dr. Zeta, this is where we need your help," Dr. Whitney pleaded, trying to move him past the linguistic confusion. They paused in the middle of the endless rows of green.

"Do you think you can you help us?"

Constant watched a bird fly by overhead.

"Are you familiar with how birds fly?"

Confused, Dr. Whitney replied trepidatiously, "I suppose their bodies evolved a means by which they were able to provide enough lift with their wings against the lightness of their frame."

"Yes, but this is only one side—they float by harmonizing with the wind, and by the grace of their creation." He paused, intuiting her intention. "Dr. Whitney, I'm sure you are well aware of the technological embargo on Egolsia. I am not in the habit of disobeying the interstellar community and providing technology to a race that has proven it is simply not ready for it. My method, which is why I thought I was here, is to engage in dialogue through Contact on a social level, through which a culture might see a more civilized possibility of living."

Dr. Whitney's body unconsciously stiffened, despite her effort to appear neutral.

"Dr. Zeta, we get ahead of ourselves here. Look, there is an assembly meeting tonight—please come, at least, hear us out."

"I will do what I can." Constant bowed cordially.

"That's all I ask," Dr. Whitney replied.

They both remounted their horses and continued their ride. The orange hills were beginning to flare under the first rays of the setting sun. They rode in the silence of the desert, each quiet in thought.

* * *

As he walked back to his quarters that night, Constant weighed the contents of his long afternoon with Dr.

Whitney. He was eager to help and still hopefully able to prove his approach could be successful, but more and more it appeared the conditions on the planet were unraveling at such an alarming rate that each possibility he was able to conceive of was quickly met with its likely futility.

It was also becoming increasingly clear that these were a people who fully believed that if their circumstances were changed, if they could just figure out the right technology, their problems would be solved. Constant did not see it this way, nor did his contemporaries, but he did believe, unlike many others, that certain forms of Contact could allow a developing species to find another way.

This theory on Contact, and the controversy surrounding it, was ironically what had caught the attention of the very people in front of which he was soon to appear. Now, however, he had a growing suspicion that it was the controversy itself that had attracted them, and not his theory—i.e., he feared that they believed he was merely some sort of maverick, who, if they played enough upon his sympathy, could be convinced to break the sanctions set in place by the Collective. If this were true, then he had made a mistake in coming here.

He sent for Owvi and Stantish to meet him at his dwelling to prepare for the meeting. They both showed up with their new Egolsian counterparts, whom Constant had to politely dismiss. He communicated his thoughts and fears to them, and while they each had their own perspectives, they all agreed that they would not make hast with a response; they had all quickly grown affection for these Egolsians, but could not let their better judgment be swayed by it.

New friends

The sun had set, and soon an escort arrived at their door. The group collected themselves, concluding their last minute thoughts with each other. There was an electric heaviness in the air, and they were all a bit uneasy. Constant smoothed his suit front, took a deep breath, and followed the escort, with his team in tow, out into the night.

Chapter 10

The Assembly

The doors opened from within, sending a warm light into the cool evening air. Constant and his comrades stepped into what was apparently a meeting in progress. Several people who had just been talking over each other simultaneously stopped and turned their attention to the newcomers. The air in there too was thick and charged. They heard the last few heated words bellowed by the freshly returned Ambassador Able.

"…and now, now our country is up for sale!" he boomed from the front of the room, dabbing his sweating forehead with a delicate piece of cloth, his back still turned to the new arrivals.

A hush fell over the crowd as they all turned to watch Constant and his team tentatively moving down the center aisle. They all silently rose in an awkward sign of respect.

"Dr. Zeta! Come in!" Dr. Whitney called out to them, seeing them now approaching. She rose from her seat at the head table and walked quickly toward them with her arms cordially outstretched.

"Please, please, here—" she followed, taking Constant by the arm and leading him to the center of the room. For Constant it was an albeit warm, but oddly formal greeting coming from someone he had just spent the day with. He felt as if she were performing it more for the room than for him, as if to cue those gathered there of Constant and his team's importance.

All eyes watched as Constant and his crew were lead to the center of the space. A buzz still hung in the air; there was an obvious restraint to continue the excited discourse that had paused when they walked in the room. Moreover, there was a profound fascination for many of them that had never seen anyone who was not from their planet. Some who, even with the de facto confirmation of their trusted colleagues, found it hard to believe in their existence—even now, when confronted with their physical forms.

And yet here they were: beings from another world. And ones upon which many of them had placed their last hopes. Constant's tall, stately manner, with his shock white hair and orange eyes, certainly was a sight to behold, but he could have easily been mistaken for a very tall, striking specimen of Nordic persuasion. Stantish blended completely, despite his traditionally tribal fashion—most of them had already wrongly assumed he was a terrestrial colleague of Storm and were now trying to reconcile their assumption.

Owvi's appearance, on the other hand, was entirely foreign to them. His physiognomy was vaguely reminiscent of many of the images they had seen in their popular culture—what Constant had surmised was actually a somewhat comic depiction of the not-so-amusing OoCulay. But to their surprise, Owvi was much more soft and 'human.' Some suppressed the urge to touch him as he walked by.

The three stood at the front of the room, surrounded by the dim light and perfect attention of the crowd. Constant was in his element. All the faces before him, gleaming with their thousands of years of history, their traditions and tribulations, their unconscious desire to know more about the universe. This is where he had constructed his living, and his academic identity, and what was now perhaps becoming his life's work, this was the moment: Contact.

"Friends!" He leveled confidently at the group before him, spreading his arms out wide in heartfelt welcome. Their stunned presence prohibited a natural response. Dr. Whitney stepped forward.

"Comrades! Allow me to introduce Dr. Constant Zeta and his colleagues. They have traveled many millions of miles—light years I should say—to be here."

The crowd instantly broke their hypnosis and clapped their hands together simultaneously in order to make a big noise, as was their custom. A few of them stepped forward to embrace Constant's hand. He and his team had each endured many such awkward ceremonies before on other planets and took it all in stride.

"Please, please, all. I know there is much to discuss, so let us begin." Extricating them from the excitement, Dr. Whitney led them around the tables, that had ceremoniously been placed at the front, to three chairs in the center that had been reserved for them. The other council members nodded cordially as they took their place. All others sat in unison and ended their commotion as quickly as they had started it.

"Let's begin." Dr. Whitney spoke with a new seriousness, looking to her right and left at the council members. Constant smiled in turn, unsure what was visibly about to brim over from the crowd, but eager to begin his initial dialogue with the people of Egolsia.

"Dr. Zeta," first began a dark-haired woman to whom he had not yet been introduced. "We are so happy that you are here. We have so many questions, and so little time, so forgive me if I get right to it. But first—" She paused, looking at the piles of papers before her, then set them down, scanning the crowd. "Ambassador Able here was just informing us of the dire situation in our capital. Ambassador Able, would you like to fill our guests in on what you were telling all of us, to help give some context for this meeting?"

Ambassador Able's rosy face puffed and wheezed as he labored to stand back up.

"Of course, of course. Dr. Zeta—friends—you see, there is no better way to say it other than our National Federation, our central government, is being formally dissolved." A heated murmur passed over the crowd. "Please, please— let me finish. You see Dr. Zeta, I believe you knew there was a coup—or at least an attempted one. Since then, the corporate conglomerate that was backing our government has pulled their support. Apparently, there was an attempt at a hostile takeover, but our President—in an unexpected moment of conscience—vetoed the action and the whole thing fell apart." He chuckled, then continued, remembering himself. "The Representatives of our Statehoods have left the capital. The military has temporarily suspended its operations. It is chaos," he sighed. The room was silent this time.

"Luckily," he continued, "the Statehoods appear for the moment to have agreed to try to run themselves, independent from the central leadership. We shall soon see how this plays out, but in the meantime—you see what little time we did have is now almost gone." He nodded in punctuation and retook his seat without waiting for a response.

The audience sat in an awkwardly pregnant silence, perhaps having anticipated a longer preamble in which to compose their thoughts, or simply thrown by the interruption of a moment ago. Either way, they all just sat there. Maybe they were hesitant to put their thoughts out there before an unknown entity from another world. A cough mercifully broke the silence.

Dr. Whitney craned, eager for someone to speak. "Alban, yes, you wish to speak?" The crowd cocked their heads in relief, placing their emotional energy on a dark figure in the back row. A gray wreathed figure stood, tugging on the tails of his worn jacket.

"Yea, I do," he replied straightening himself. It was one of the elder practical engineers, a man of broad stature and many years.

"Dr. Zeta," he drew. "Welt that's all nice and pretty about er Gov'nent," he said shooting a glance at Ambassador Able, before continuing, "but it seems ta me, the lights are aboot to go out in this here country, and that means trouble for us all. Trouble for this land, trouble for the people of this here planet." He pressed, then spurred on by his breaking of the silence. "We need energy, energy to keep these lights on. Energy to keep the power on. Ya see energy is light for us... and light is power."

A number of acknowledgments peppered the tops of the crowd with "here here" and "it's true." He continued, gaining steam.

"Light here means order ya see. It binds us. Without it, the people, they... they can't see. They don't feel safe. They can't work. They can't watch their screens. It's chaos really. They don't care 'bout the Federation. It's long since done nothing for us. Good riddance to it. It's light, it's light though—Light is the peg that holds our world together." He paused, looking into his hands. "We need you to show us. We need you to hep' us keep those lights on sir. Or, or we're doomed."

His head dropped in profound punctuation as a lush but polite burst of applause tore over the crowd, which quickly, however, passed to expectant smiles.

Through the smoke and warm glare of the room, all eyes, including Dr. Whitney's, fell expectantly on Constant. He smiled warmly and rose.

"Friends. Friend—and what is it that you are called sir?

"Alban sir," he replied proudly.

"Alban, I am here to help you see other possibilities, to enter a cultural dialogue, to find a way to effect change through the example of other peoples, not to bestow technological advances. Now, if I may—"

"But we can't wait!" Another audience member shot up. "If our country collapses, then there's nothing to discuss!"

"I understand. However, it is not necessarily about the

present state of things that you should be focused. Ideas take time to find their rooting. It is part of the natural way of things for civilizations to die and be reborn—"

"With all due respect Dr. Zeta," another broke in, rising with an obvious heat. "I can say with the assurance of all here that we do indeed work for the future, but if this country descends into a state of complete chaos, we will have no ways in which to disseminate the new solutions that we have been so tirelessly developing here, so our plans for the future will be then null and void. If society reverts, and we lose the center, then we will become sucked into a spiral of damage control and end up simply trying to survive," he concluded, sinking back as if exhausted by the statement.

"Yes, I understand your people's need for continuity," Constant replied, trying to hang on. "However, I believe there is also a myth of your people's which demonstrates the rebirth of civilization through the story of the Phoenix. It is sometimes necessary for society to reach an ashen state before it is able to grow anew—"

"Are you suggesting we simply allow our entire culture to collapse?!" he shot back, popping back up with an incredulous heat in his tone and his eye.

Constant smiled benevolently. "Well, possibly, yes. You might not have a choice."

Cries of disbelief and disapproval flared up from the crowd, along with their ire and equal passion. Arguments broke out between those who had finally risen to join the discussion just as it had descended to an impasse, perhaps at the same point Constant had found them when he had first walked into the room.

"Please, please, everyone!" Frank and Dr. Whitney shouted to their compatriots, banging the table with a large ceremonial wooden hammer.

"Stop!" Frank boomed with a magnanimous but severe tone of startling command. The crowd reluctantly turned their attention back to the front of the room. Frank turned to Constant, his tone dropping to a soft sincerity.

"Dr. Zeta, you'll have to forgive us—we are living in desperate times, and so sometimes we forget ourselves. The thing is, we brought you here to help us—can you help us?"

"I—," no sooner had he opened his mouth than shouts from outside and a tremendous crash broke the tense air of the room. Several small cracks followed.

Storm and Stantish simultaneously jumped up from their chairs, as Storm shouted to the crowd:

"Bandits!"

Chapter 11

The desperate

Chaos had broken out. Storm flew out of the door, closely followed by Frank, who swept up the crowd as he went, like birds following a leader. Stantish and Dr. Whitney quickly led Constant, with Owvi in tow, down a dirt staircase at the back of the tent. Shouts and flashing shadows added a confusing shroud to their egress, and by the time they made it down to an underground corridor which led to a small junction hall, Constant was completely turned around. They stopped to collect themselves, and Stantish quickly corralled the group.

"Constant, the most secure location on the compound is at the front wall, though it is from there that they will direct their defensive—but it is also from there where they will most likely launch their offensive. I recommend we instead fall back to the dwelling in which you are quartered. It is not as secure, but well defensible, and less likely to be attacked."

"I want to observe." Constant quickly directed back.

"Fine. Owvi, please see Dr. Whitney back to her quarters," Stantish said, turning now to Owvi.

"Oh, I'm going to too." Dr. Whitney replied. "This way," she pointed.

And with that they were following her through the darkly lit tunnel system, heading toward the front wall.

Following the sounding of the alarm, many of the community's inhabitants had either gathered at their stations in the bunker or at defensible positions throughout the compound. As they approached the bunker, a cacophony of shouting voices echoed off the damp underground walls ahead. The air was wet and electric with fear and purpose. Constant felt his pulse rise with each footfall. He hated violence, but he was becoming aware of a slightly intoxicating feeling caused by the threat of the situation. Dr. Whitney quickly ushered them through the large iron door, before slamming it shut with a loud bang.

There was something of a controlled pandemonium happening in the bunker. As they stepped down in its wide, circular control deck, people ran this way and that, some shouting orders, others racing to follow them. From a distance it appeared as sheer chaos, yet the atmosphere was of intense concentration, and nothing was betrayed in their movements but the ease of previously orchestrated dance. It seemed to Constant that, whether by practice or by trial, they had done this before, and if they were afraid, they were not showing it now.

In the middle of it all stood Frank, like an immovable spindle around which all things turned. He was concentrating intently on a map on the table, to which he pointed

out a location to two others that stood by him. They nodded
and immediately disembarked. He had not looked up when
Constant and his crew had entered the room, but he briefly
did so now, and then returned to his work, motioning them
over with his hand.

"Please, sit. You will be safe here." Frank gestured to a set
of low benches next to them.

"If it is all the same to you, we wish to observe, and help if
we can," Stantish replied, attempting to catch his eye.

Frank looked back at him. "Storm is at the front of the
wall. I'm sure he would value your assistance." Stantish
glanced at Constant, who nodded in affirmation, and in an
instant he was gone.

The remaining crew gathered around Frank as he did his
best to brief them on what exactly was happening, while
intermittently dispensing orders to his deputies, who darted
in, reported, got direction, and departed like hummingbirds
feeding on a blossoming flower.

The attack, he believed, was coming from a nomadic band
of raiders that they had encountered before. An advance
group had somehow passed the Grand Mile undetected,
gotten through the main gate, and failed at what they
assumed had meant to be a clandestine forward attack,
by immediately trying to smash their way into the guard
station, ostensibly to open the front gate. They had since
been subdued. Now, however, there was a much larger group
crossing the Grand Mile, and a few advancing very quickly
in vehicles. Storm was at the front of the wall, preparing a
defense to engage them as soon as they were in range.

They believed that the attackers were composed of two

groups, which they surmised had recently merged. They regularly scouted the surrounding area and had a few weeks prior caught site of a smaller group camping 3 days journey from the South side of the Mountains that flanked the far end of the Grand Mile. They lost sight of them over the last few days and had assumed they had moved on. Most travelers did.

Most of their neighbors had recently left too. There were a few families that had stayed, digging into their ancestral soil and embracing a quiet and limited society composed of only those that they knew had stayed behind. They mostly kept to themselves. The only beings that found their business on the plain were inevitably nomadic, moving through one increasingly desolate region after another, pausing only to rally themselves against a potential target to be pillaged, before moving onto the next location.

As a consequence there still remained a few large marauding bands that swept up and down the plains, presiding over it, forever hunting and rooting through the impotent land. These were the really dangerous ones. It was as if they had been waiting all their lives for this—almost as if the thinnest barrier of society had prevented them from descending into their true form—savage—and when it was lifted they sprung into their new life with equal parts fervor and desperation.

It was Frank's fear that one of these clans had churned up a larger nomadic group, and had focused them on the objective of dissembling their encampment for resources. At least this is how it appeared to them as they scanned the horizon from their embrasures, dust clouds kicking and billowing from the fervent band that was now tearing across the desert, with their sights clearly set on the front gate.

Two deputy commanders had returned from outdoors to report back to Frank. He did not look happy at the news. Excusing himself, he left without hesitation, leaving the three of them to their own devices.

Unsure about what to do, Constant, Dr. Whitney, and Owvi were now confronted with whether to get involved or wait in safety while all others risked their lives. Their discussion was brief—despite all three of their objections to violence—they decided to join the others at the front of the wall.

* * *

Angry billows of dust swirled up from the scorched floor of the plain, like a massive war flag, silently thundering their approach. There were two fast-modified vehicles leading the charge from far affront, clad haphazardly in scavenged sheets of metal, dusted gray and red with rust. Behind them slowly followed another vehicle, towering and monstrous, something that looked more like a moving cumulation of metal buildings than a transport. At every edge, multiple figures seemed to be protruding from it, riding as if it were a monolithic beast. Flanking this lumbering terrestrial ship, were several random gangs, some atop horses, some running together in splotchy clusters. The whole dark pile swelled toward them across the flatland, slowly and silently, with a quiet fury.

Constant handed the field glass back to Storm. It was an unnerving sight. The air outside was electric, like in that silver-metallic moment before a storm. Inside, the atmosphere was thin and heavy, as if all the oxygen had been sucked out of the room. Everyone in the bunker braced themselves. Constant felt again that strange sickly sweet sense of excitement. He did not like it. Or perhaps he did not like that there was some part of him that did in fact like it. He loathed violence, yet was becoming more aware of the corrosive intoxication of it. He was aware of the deadly nature of the current situation, but it still seemed somewhat difficult to grasp that in this quiet place there was potential for such injury. It all felt so unreal.

Owvi sensed his conflict and placed his hand on Constant's arm, looking up with a soft-eyed empathy. "These beings are desperate Constant. There are a few who are driven by malice, but for the rest, it is only a cover for their fear. Do not worry." He squeezed his arm.

This was not the first time Constant and Owvi had been in a grave situation together, and neither was it the first time he was a comfort to him. It was arguable whether the Wvio's strong proclivity for empathy rendered them more vulnerable, or even could be construed as naive, but all the same, they had an uncanny ability to intuit the motivations of their enemies. As such, they were rarely afraid. This afforded them a singular perspective when they had found themselves in battle, and steadied them in situations they might otherwise find untenable.

All the same, Constant was nervous. He was nervous for Dr. Whitney and her compatriots and nervous for the mission, which seemed to rise in stakes in inverse proportion to its likelihood of success. He wrung his hands and did not answer Owvi. He took the glass from Storm and once again surveyed the horizon. They were coming on fast.

"Any moment now," Storm spoke softly in his ears.

The gray-black-inky mass swelled and spread, the dark tentacles of its flanks wound their way over the low dunes. The point of it was now more sharply defined by the lead vehicles, as it plunged across the heat distorted horizon, closer and closer into focus.

"On your mark!" Storm boomed back to his rank, lined in attention at the narrow windows. They all simultaneously set their stance and squinted into their sights. Not a breath broke the air. "NOW!" shouted Storm.

In an instant, the dune runners broke over the ridge of the far plateau, and popped silently into the air, flipping and flying apart at the moment right after a deep boom reverberated within the walls of the bunker. The crack of explosives was heard right after the hillside lit up, riveted with projectiles. Pinprick white flashes popped and whizzed about the hulking body of the large carrier. Several of the figures that had been clinging to its sides fell easily to the ground, like mites sloughing off the back of some great beast.

It accelerated with a heave, its massive wheels spinning and twisting against the desert floor. There was a pause in the chaotic cracking of the projectiles as the men inside the wall quickly reloaded their weapons. In this moment the roar of the great beast's combustion engine finally echoed against the wall, and the reality of its imminent arrival finally hit all of them stationed there at the front. Storm ordered all of them to get down.

Bucking forward and back like a rampaging quadruped, the ship finally lurched forward, smashing and crashing into the front gate, and halted with a tremendous grind that shook the entire contents of the bunker. Now suddenly inert, steam viscously erupted from the evil grin of its patch-work grill and poured from all sides of its mangled head.

Dozens of dusty, ragged, and heavily outfitted figures rushed from its crevices, abandoning the dying vessel. Most were armed with primitive and improvised weapons, which they swung wildly in a successful effort to appear terrify-ing. No sooner did they hit the ground than they headed directly for the face of the wall, climbing with an agility that their rustic appearance did not betray, disappearing from Constant's vantage point above.

Almost instantly several reappeared, tumbling backward onto the desert floor. Crackling shots from above punc-tured them as they fell, popping and tearing at their clothes. Two now lay lifeless right before their window. It took a moment for Constant to comprehend what he was seeing. Owvi moaned.

Two small children ran up to a couple of the fallen and, wasting not a moment, grabbed them by their heals and began pulling them back towards the shipwrecked carrier. They did not seem for a moment to notice that one of the figure's faces had been partially removed by the blast of a projectile. The figure was hard to make out, but it appeared to be a young woman by her long black hair, which now was being dragged through the bloody dust.

The desperate

Constant began to feel sick to his stomach. It was not only the death that he had just witnessed, but the coldness with which this group seemed to carry out their mission, and the earnest precision with which they where now being repelled. It did not speak well for either side.

More attackers now approached, climbing over the steaming hulk of the carrier and through the hole it had dug in the gate. Constant could hear shouts from above. He saw Storm suddenly appear at the gate with an antique rifle, holding it by the barrel. He swung it squarely at one of the intruder's heads, knocking it back at a sickening angle. Constant heard the crack of the impact. Several more intruders swarmed the gate, forcing Storm back. The loud successive boom of artillery shivered the hall. Things were escalating quickly.

"I've seen enough," Constant concluded, Owvi nodding in unison.

He glanced at Stantish, who immediately whisked him along, with Owvi and Dr. Whitney, back down the damp hallway and across the camp's center circle to Constant's lodging. They secured themselves without incident, and from that vantage point, they watched the sad demise of the desperate attackers, who set themselves so fiercely against the encampment. The battle lasted until the early morning, as the stragglers were worn down and the runners were chased back deep enough into the desert.

* * *

The next morning was studied and quiet. The mist had

returned and hung about the scene of the previous night's fray with a melancholy indifference. Gray and silver-washed were all the still figures strewn about the compound, splashed with a red-brown, as if with the caprice of a macabre artist. Few spoke as they went about their work, and those who did, did so in a hushed tone. The bodies of the intruders were being disposed of with an unhurried deliberateness. The rest moved from repair to repair, punctuating the air with the intermittent smack of a hammer or buzz of a saw.

Constant and Owvi sat quietly on the porch of the lodging house and surveyed the scene, lost in contemplation. Dr. Whitney and Stantish had jointly gone down to help with the cleanup, but they had stayed behind, both deeply affected by what had transpired the night before.

There they spent the day, occasionally replying out loud to each other's thoughts with one word answers. It was late afternoon before Constant finally stood up and announced to Owvi that he would be going into the desert.

After informing Dr. Whitney of his plans, several orderlies had been sent to help make preparations for him. A pack was drawn up, then lightened after he refused the use of a horse. He said that he needed to be alone. He had assured them that he was more than capable of handling himself on such walks. It was them he was worried about.

Shortly before sunset, he walked out onto the western plain, alone and unarmed, carrying only the small pack of provisions. His serenely moving figure grew smaller as the light grew dimmer until he was swallowed by the darkness of the desert.

Chapter 12

Constant's vision in the desert

It was exquisite. The sun was beginning to slowly drop behind the distant desert mountains, sending streaks of color across the dome of the sky, the likes of which Constant had never seen before. Deep hues one might think to find in the most exotic of flowers, the kind that one had to travel many moons to the basin of some galactically remote rain-forest to see, were now all gloriously strewn about the sky. It was like some molecular river's edge, so laden with gold that it overflowed onto its bank.

Constant smiled. Things were not going well.

It was looking more and more like his doubters were right. He did consider the possibility that the beings of this planet were totally insane. His instincts, however, told him they were not, or at least not irrevocably. He felt shame at the thought. But what else was he to conclude? They lived in by far the most beautiful planet that he had ever visited, yet were in an almost constant state of misery.

There was a certain sweetness to them that he could not explain, but it was very difficult to cognate this when considering their extensive history with, and seemingly endless capacity for, violence. This fact he had just borne witness to.

Still, he wanted to help them. He needed to help them— if only for himself. He thought it was perhaps selfish of him to think this way, but he couldn't help it. He found himself unable to separate his own interests, his own desire to prove himself and his ideas here on this very planet, from his basic instinct to help another being, born of the Great Spirit, who was in trouble. It all might not matter though, he thought to himself, because he was not sure if he was even able to do it.

They wanted what they were not ready for. Their demand, their desperation for it alone was proof enough. Still, what were they to do? They could not grasp what could be a needed part of the process of their existence on this planet, and in fact, every planet: that is, the periodic death and rebirth of civilizations.

The planetary tribes of the Lodi Arcurii, for example, followed a strict celestial calendar, by which they planned the end of each of their great ages. They quietly and solemnly burned their cities to the ground and then returned to the forests for the course of three full generations, before reemerging and starting again. More advanced civilizations, however, foresaw the coming end of each great age and prepared for a transition hundreds of years ahead of time, encapsulating all the knowledge of their time in a new form that could be retained by the new generation.

It would not be the first time this happened to Egolsia. They had lost their knowledge before. In fact, they were still completely unaware of a substantial portion of their own history, that even now lay asleep at the bottom of their oceans. They had been here before, they would be here again—if they were lucky.

And so, he saw their predicament—they did not want their world to end. And their fears were justified. The situation on their planet was becoming more and more untenable. Their weather systems had become completely unbalanced, making it almost impossible to live anywhere without all kinds of artificial aides. Their relationship to energy and their obsession with killing each other made it quite difficult for any outside agency, especially one such as humble as himself, to help them. Still, he could not let go of the belief that he could. It meant everything to him. He could not imagine returning home now, with all of his dissenters proven correct. He had to find another way.

The sun had now set, and the fading light was giving one last show of rich blue shades. He sat down on the edge of an outcropping of rock, overlooking the vast plain stretching out before him, and took in its grandeur. The desert was cooling and quieting, though the night's occupants were now starting to stir. A speckled silence hung about the valley like a vast hushed note. He contemplated.

One of the most difficult things for him to grasp about the beings of this planet was their sense of separateness. Here in this valley, the low buzz of the Energy-of-All-Things flowed through everything with an ineffable bareness. It was so evident here on this plain, why did they not see it?

Enraptured, he gave himself over to the valley. It opened to him and he slowly sank in. He heard all the night creatures now beginning their chorus to the twilight. The movement of life entered him and took him over each rock and passed him through every crevasse. He swept the desert, and the breeze moved over and through him. The night began its song, and the moon made its grand entrance, shining out over the valley with its crisp ethereal light.

There was an ancient spirit here. He could feel it. There were a people who once lived here, who were a part of this land. This land knew itself; it was shy but ready to talk. It was vast and harsh, but ready to listen. It had reigned grandly for thousands of years, and would continue to reign for many thousand more to come—snowstorms and heat waves be damned.

The spirits of the valley now drew him out. He saw the energy of the desert turn like a spindle on the floor of the plain. The wheel in the sky turned, and by it, all things were charged and driven. He saw its architecture, its eternal dance. The spirits mingled with the cactus flowers. The molecules of the valley danced in unison. The desert was revealing itself to him, like one of its lonely flowers.

He saw a vision of the energy-of-all-things turning and coursing through all of the life around him. He saw the axis on which the whole great nature turned. It was in this moment he had an epiphany. It was from here, this great well, this great river, from which they could draw life, draw the energy that they needed, without upsetting the balance of their Nature. They need only find a way to tap into it, something to simply capture its flow, something like an antenna—

The desert night carried him on through his vision, and throughout the night he remained there. He sat softly in its tranquility. He listened to its secrets. He did not sleep till morning, until the first rays of dawn finally broke his peace.

Chapter 13

Decisions

The next morning, Constant returned to camp quietly and unhurried. He immediately went to his quarters without a word and sent for Owvi. There, the two sequestered themselves, talking into the night and for the following two days, discussing the ideas that had come to Constant during his respite in the desert.

Dr. Whitney, though preoccupied with the repair of the camp as all the others were, did stop in to check on the two of them when their meals, which they often refused, were brought to them. She did not get much from them. Tii also had visited them, but only made it as far as the porch before stopping in front of the door, smiling a knowing smile, and turning and leaving as softly as she came.

Stantish had taken over another employ. Since the night of the attack, he and Storm had begun to strategize what to do about this now looming threat. The assault had been a massive blow to their morale and had shaken the core of the camp's sense of security. It had shown them that their very existence was now threatened.

There were three fatalities and twelve wounded, and a number of those were seriously injured. Most of the wounded had been hit by projectiles and were now waiting their turn to have the offending objects extracted from their bodies. The three fatalities had been caused by a fire that broke out in the shed that they were using for cover.

The camp itself had sustained some damage—though not as extreme as it could have been—save for their gate, that still lay under the crashed vehicle which had felled it. The vehicle was the only thing that had been left behind by the intruders, and only because it was quite stuck where it was. A group of engineers were currently dismantling it for any useful parts, as well as inspecting it for any information about their attackers.

From Storm's perspective—other than the deaths of their people—the greatest loss exacted by this attack was their loss of secrecy. The intruders who had made it inside of the wall and escaped had carried back with them the verification of the existence of the camp, as well as its basic contents. Even though the camp's inhabitants had shown their strength in defending it, the encounter had still given the attackers a view of its great value, if they were able to try again and succeed at taking it.

And so, a certain unease had begun to pervade over the camp. Storm and Stantish did not believe this should stand, nor did they believe they should passively wait to find out if it would happen again. After a lengthy discussion, they concluded that the only appropriate response was to pursue the villains and make sure they would not be able to launch such an offensive on them again—or at least, force them to lose their appetite for it.

Together, they planned their pursuit. Frank was overwhelmed with caring for the injured and trying to repair the camp, so he entrusted them with the decision of how to handle the attackers. They had assembled a group in the center court and were now deliberating the best method to track down the fleeing party that hopefully had paused somewhere in the nearby desert in order to regroup. They decided to break up in teams of two, each heading off in a different direction. Stantish and Storm would take the camp's fastest vehicle, which in this case was the dune runner that Constant and his team had come in on, and the rest would go on horseback.

The plan was for the two taking the dune runner to cross the Grand Mile directly and connect up to the old highway, pursuing it as far as they could. If the bandits had taken this route, it might be possible for them to catch up to them. More likely, they were camping in the scrubby hills due south of the encampment. Their aim was to first locate the group, then rendezvous with the others to decide what to do based on what they discovered.

Even as they prepared to embark, there was still debate on what they would do once they found them. Storm was ready for retaliation. Stantish was still uncertain. Under normal circumstances, he was always prepared to pursue more diplomatic pursuits of peace, long before he would ever consider violence. But here, he felt, the stakes were too high. He had been quite attached to these Egolsians, and felt for their plight, and based on what he had seen in the desperation of the marauders, he did not believe that they could be reasoned with—or trusted.

The rest of the group was split. Those for retaliation agreed with them and believed that for their safety they must hunt and kill the marauders because, even if they didn't return themselves for another raid, they could easily pass on the details about the community, and inspire another attack from a different traveling crew.

Those who opposed such violence said that it stood against the principles of their community, and the ideals which they wished to instill as the foundation for a new tomorrow. They could not bear the thought of creating another society predicated on violent acts. That had not, in the unfolding of time, worked before. Others argued that what they were seeking to defend itself had been gained originally through violent means, and had forever cursed them. It was further arguable that that specific notion contributed heavily to the predicament they were now in: progress above all.

This gave Stantish pause. None among them knew this more deeply than him—it was part of his heredity. His people had suffered deeply for eons, embroiled in warfare which spanned planets and solar systems, though they had not grasped the extent of their torment at the time. They were at one point celebrated as the bravest and most feared people in their galactic quadrant. They had mastered the art of war, but this had been at a price. Their people had dwindled, and their values had twisted to eventually serve only that master. Nearing what seemed to some as their final hour, they had concluded that the true aim of War was not domination—that pursuit was poison—but it was in fact peace. Thus, if they pursued peace directly, they would be able to transcend war. And so they did.

It was this hereditary knowledge that now came into direct conflict with what Stantish was experiencing here on Egolsia. He too had felt the same sensations of excitement that Constant had experienced at the inception of the attack of the marauders, only, due to his nature, ten-fold in comparison. He was however aware of the dangers of following these types of impulses. It was not that his people considered these instincts bad, or wrong, only "not the way to peace" as he had heard so many times in his childhood.

And now this was all at odds with his current impulses to protect his colleagues, in which he now included Storm and the rest of the camp, at any cost. He knew in his bones that violence could not bear fruit to a long-term positive outcome, but the fact of the moment was that they were vulnerable, and could possibly lose everything if they did not do something. And the surest method of defense in this case, by his coldest calculations, was a direct offense. And one that needed to happen now.

There was something else he could not put his finger on, that was undoubtedly influencing his thought process, but he knew not how. It was as if the planet's inhabitants generated an atmosphere that produced a stimulation of violent tendencies. Since he had been here, spending time amongst the Egolsians, he had noticed an undercurrent, an influence, an agitation, a propensity towards this line of action—it inhabited so much of their reality that it caused a sphere of influence that enveloped everyone into it. Case in point: he at times found himself easily losing his temper, and even on occasion had a hard time focusing.

All of this weighed on him as the others waited for him to cast his vote. He felt he could not take the risk: it was not his risk to take. He voted to go on the offensive against their attackers, but only if it seemed necessary.

As they prepared to go, he reassured himself that he need not worry yet, as their first goal was just to find them, and then find any information about them that they could. Then they would make the call—and he would try to avoid violence at all costs.

And so Stantish left the camp with his team, in this cloud of dust and conflict. And it was just then that Constant and Owvi finally descended from the boarding house. They had called to Dr. Whitney to assemble the council. They had a solution.

Chapter 14

Plans

"We will build it together," Constant began.

He was pacing intently on his porch steps. The council was now just taking their seats in the front row, and a hush fell over the crowd. Dr. Whitney and Frank, along with anyone else in the camp who could be spared from their duties, had gathered on the lawn in front of Constant's lodging. They were all eager with anticipation as to what he had to say.

"We will build it together," he repeated, "and we will teach you how." He was very excited. And so was Owvi, so much so he almost showed it.

In the front, Constant observed Frank's face relax with relief. Constant quickly responded.

"Oh, no, my apologies Frank. It is not cold fusion. In retrospect, I should have led with that. Let me start over."

Constant collected himself, while Owvi regained his normal placid state.

"Friends. Two nights ago in the desert, I had a vision. In

it, I saw something which has provided us with a possible solution. When the technological embargo was placed on Egolsia by the interstellar community, it was centered on keeping solar level energy out of the hands of the power possessors of this planet for fear that it would be used for the purposes of war, especially the inter-planetary exportation of war.

"And I must admit to my own conflict over this subject. It is no secret my theories on Contact are held in controversy—though I also recognize that the disproportionate Egolsian hunger for powerful energy sources is troubling insofar as it is quite clear that—and please pardon any offense—your race has not developed far enough past its violent tendencies to be trusted with them."

A muddled murmur passed over the crowd, but immediately ceased when Dr. Whitney turned around. Constant continued without noticing.

"However, the desert that surrounds us has revealed to me a possible solution. In the desert, I saw how the energy you seek is, in fact, all around us all the time. It is the energy that turns the planet, that moves the clouds, that awakens all the creatures of the desert in the morning. It breathes life into the plants and sends them soaring toward the moon at night.

"So it was there that it struck me: is it possible to harness that energy? It is an eternal energy, but a terrestrial one, and finds its boundaries here within the atmosphere of Egolsia. So Owvi and I—mostly Owvi—have found a way to tap into that energy field, and to capture and channel it in a way that you will be able to replicate."

He paused, looking around at the somewhat confused faces that surrounded him.

"It's like your windmills, only moved by the energy that moves not only the wind but the planet itself," Constant clarified. The crowd shuffled about in awkward silence, still not quite grasping.

Constant smiled. "We are going to show you how to build a generator."

* * *

Over the next few weeks, Constant and Owvi laid out the plans for the generator in meticulous detail. Tii and rest of the engineering department worked closely with them to document everything, trying to grasp as much as possible, for it would be on them to someday relate these plans and help others construct it again. There was a hush about the camp. Even those who were not directly aiding in this process felt responsible; should this work, it would mean the experiment of the community itself was a success, and moreover, that they might provide to their people a solution to a problem that had all but consumed them.

The generator would be constructed of three main parts: a lower component that was submerged under the surface of the planet, a larger upper component which extended upward in a reciprocal distance, and a central component at the ground level that mediated between the two.

The lower component would start with a deep cylindrical hole being dug into the ground. Then, the inside would be coated and sealed with clay to the degree that it was watertight, and then filled with water. Submerged within it would be a number of monolithic blocks of stone, intermittently wrapped with copper wire. The chamber would then be sealed by a large heavy plate with an aperture in the center, through which a braid of copper wire would pass.

The upper component would be composed of several thick plates of iron that would be arranged in two opposing groups: the inner and the outer. Both groups were attached to a center pole, and swung at perpendicular angles to each other, creating a gyroscopic effect. Like the monoliths, the plates were wrapped with copper wire at varying lengths and widths.

The central component was the most magic of all. It was composed mainly of copper, except for a few structural elements that attached it to the frame of the structure. It was shaped like a large coupling, which receded toward the center, reciprocally on the top and bottom, into a bell-cone shape which never quite found the other side. The fulcrum at which the center pole met it, and upon which it spun, was a realization of the figure Constant had seen in his vision. It represented the aperture through which the sky poured into the Earth, and the Earth into plants and animals—it was the nexus of heaven and Earth, the place where the great magical handoff of energy between these worlds happened, the valve through which the vast universe pumped energy into Egolsia itself, sending it spinning into life.

Taken together, the whole structure was more of an "antenna" to the magnetic planetary energy field than an actual generator, Constant explained, but the term would serve their purpose, as would the energy it would generate.

Plans

The one they were planning to make would not only power their compound and all of its equipment, but potentially several small Egolsian towns.

It was terrestrial but still powerful. It was not the nuclear fusion that happened in the heart of the sun, but the hum and harmony of life on planet Egolsia itself, powerful enough on its own level. It could sustain life as it was needed—it could "keep the lights on," as Engineer Alban would say—and also allow them room for the judicious use of technology to further the practical knowledge, as well as the comfort, of their species. And it could do this in a way that could be difficult for their power possessors to control.

None, especially Constant, thought this was the solution to all of their problems. Those ran much too deep inwardly to be solved by some outer invention, or change in circumstance, and they all knew that. But it did solve one problem, and that was the problem of the paradigm that used violent control and manipulation of the ill-gotten energy source that powered their overly comfortable lives. It was a chance to live outside that prison they had all so unwittingly placed themselves in.

It was also a chance for Constant to prove his theory of Contact to the Galactic scientific community. He knew that what he was doing here was questionable, though he was—to the best that he and Owvi were able to determine—not explicitly breaking any of the rules of Contact founded by the Cooperative. Still, if there was any success, not only would that mean vindication for his ideas against his doubters, but also the potential for a new philosophy and study of inter-species intervention.

And so now they had a plan. And only time would reveal the answer to the one question that had been plaguing Constant this entire time: would it save them?

New Perspectives

Chapter 15

The storm arrives

The day construction was scheduled to begin a massive, rogue storm swept into the valley, burying the entire compound in snow. Dr. Whitney awoke that morning to the same disorienting white glow coming through her window that was beginning to mark such occasions with more and more frequency.

She climbed from bed, her feet gingerly hitting the usually cold floor, and strode over to the window. Her fingertips pressed against the damp window sill, as she leaned against the glass. From there she could see the entire scene of the compound serenely glittering all white in the sun. Although the sight was somewhat troubling and was no doubt going to set them back a few days, it was still beautiful. She smiled.

She walked back over to the other side of the room, catching a glimpse of her own lithe body in the mirror. She paused, adjusting herself in her gray on gray military under clothes, before continuing over to her dresser where a porcelain water pitcher and basin waited. She stripped and began washing herself with the cold, bracing water where she stood.

Water rationing meant she only took a hot bath once a week. Still, the cold water that had been set out for her was a luxury and one that she knew few people in the camp enjoyed. She was aware that she was favored with a few such luxuries, like having a living quarters all to her own. Only a couple others, such as Frank, who normally stayed in the house where Constant was boarding, and who was now temporarily staying with her neighbor the medical doctor, enjoyed the same solitude. Most of the community lived in multi-unit or more dormitory-like living quarters.

Most of these luxuries had not come at her request, however; they had been insisted upon by others in the community. Even in an intentionally self-governed community, there was still a hierarchy. It pleased them to have her cared for, as they valued her as a leader. Still, though she did enjoy her private bath from time to time, she often forewent it for the public one.

When they began rationing water, they built a public bathhouse that could sustain everyone, and once a week filled it with hot water. It was one of the few places the whole community gathered and bonded together, and she valued that over her comfort.

She finished washing and selected an identical set of gray on gray military issue under clothes. Her flex-screen on the dresser top caught her eye with a slowly pulsing soft glow. Undoubtedly there was already a discussion going on this morning as to how quickly they could dig themselves out of the tons of snow that had fallen on them during the night. She waved her hand over the device to silence it, and began her curt process of dressing, taking her work coverall from the hook where it hung.

Slapping her flex-screen on her wrist, she made her way down to the porch. From there she was able to get a closer survey of the whole scene—they were in deeper than she had first thought from the cold remove of her upper window. The entire community seemed swallowed up by the snow. People intermittently popped up like black streaks out of the white, digging out pathways in places where some of the drifts were over their heads. Machinery had been started up to aid in the process, puffing up billows of smoke here and there and sending a clacking echo through the dampened streets.

It would definitely be days before they were able to begin construction on the generator, she thought to herself. Possibly an entire week, and that was if another storm didn't follow. To be fair, they had not had one for a while, and it had given them a false notion that the ones that had plagued them last summer had been an anomaly. On that occasion, they had experienced week upon week of hail, freezing rain, and blizzards that disappeared as quickly as they came.

She heard a blustery voice calling out to her from below. It was Ambassador Able coming up the snowed over path to her house. Great plumes of breath were shooting up from his red, round face, which sat atop a tall, spherical body all cloaked in black, making him look like some great mythological creature clumsily powering its way through the snow to her doorstep.

She nimbly hopped down the steps to meet him, smiling to herself. Taking his arm, she pulled him up onto the porch, where they stopped for a moment so he could catch his breath.

"Princess Fatima is coming," he said between labored exhalations.

"What, now? Why?" Her smile cooled—she was confused.

"Yes, today," he replied. "I sent you a message this morning."

"I haven't checked them yet." She looked at him puzzled, unconsciously touching her flex-screen. "Did you know she was coming?"

He paused looking at the ground. "Well no, I only found out early this morning. I mean, I saw her when I was in Washington. She was curious to hear Constant and his team had stayed behind. She offered her help, and I told her we would keep that in mind."

She furrowed her brow, thinking. Then replied "Ambassador Able, I'm sure I don't have to tell you of the importance of discretion about what we do here. I know that Princess Fatima is supposedly a friend of this community, but even friends can have many motivations."

Ambassador Able straightened his back and took a hurt tone. "Dr. Whitney, with all due respect, I know you are suspicious of her or do not like her for whatever your reasons, but I need not remind you of the help she has given us already, and how this community may very well not exist without her efforts."

She paused and frowned, placing her hand on his shoulder.

"Yes, I know. I just find her unexpected arrival—particularly the timing—disconcerting. Especially now, with what we are about to do. Well, what do you think? How much do we tell her?"

"Let's discuss with Frank and the rest of the council. We should still have a few hours before she arrives," he replied.

"I agree," she said, taking him by the arm. "Let's go."

The two gray and black figures made their way down the white drift, disappearing into the blanketed camp below.

Chapter 16

Princess Fatima

They were all standing together waiting to greet her when she finally arrived. A large clearing had been made on the upper embankment near the solar fields so that her airship could land. It had begun to flurry again before the Princess's arrival, so her ship seemed to appear from nowhere, suddenly penetrating the white mist, pausing and then slowly hovering to a landing. The airship was slightly larger then they thought it would be, and so barely fit into the clearing.

It was quite a big thing, but without the quiet grace of the ship that Constant and his team had taken from the Mapping Station. The front portion was a massive chrome polished half moon, affixed to the front like a helmet. The back was a giant black tapered block of seemingly un-aerodynamic, crisscrossing geometry that met at the tail end before sweeping back forward in two giant prongs, like stylized bird's feet, upon which it now landed. There was a low lumbering hum to its operation, so much so that some of the snowy walls of the clearing slid in and melted under its rumbling heat.

Dr. Whitney, Ambassador Able, Frank, and the rest of the council stood wrapped in large black furs, holding them tightly against the whipping wind. A large door on the ship's underbelly opened and extended to the ground. Princess Fatima walked out first, ahead of her guard. Her vestige alone made a striking entrance. As the snow swirled all around her, the lustrous crimson of her tribal pattern embroidered cloak pierced the white of the storm. It dragged about the fallen snow, rising up to her graceful shoulders to a pointed hood, within which sat her shining ebony face. Her air was as intimidating as she was beautiful; that is to say, quite a lot. No wonder I don't like her, Dr. Whitney mused to herself, half-serious.

Her guard followed her out wearing modern winter camouflage—and they were armed. This raised a few eyebrows. She walked forward with an almost effortless air, arms warmly reaching out for them.

"Dr. Whitney! Ambassador Able! Frank! So pleasing it is to see you," she sang, smiling, with her deep honey-toned voice, as she stepped off the ramp to greet them.

"I hope my intrusion has not caused you too much fuss. Please, please," she kissed each of them three times on the cheeks, as was her custom.

"And please, do not mind them," she said, motioning dismissively to her guards. "My apologies for their stern appearance. Ever since the President stepped down, security has become so bothersome. You know, protocol." She laughed breezily.

"We are honored to have you here Princess," Frank said with his best formal tone. "Come, let's get out of the snow."

The party left together down a freshly cleared path, and the guards were left at the ship's entrance with a wave of Princess Fatima's hand.

***

They gathered at the council house, all pressed in together in the center room. They sat around a large stone fireplace, roaring with a freshly stoked fire. Hot drams were served. They exchanged pleasantries, and all settled in for what each hoped would not be a long, or awkward, discussion.

"Dr. Whitney, Ambassador Able tells me that Dr. Zeta and his team have decided to stay and that you are potentially working on some exciting things with them. Would you be so kind as to tell me about them?"

Dr. Whitney flashed Ambassador Able a hot glance, which he expertly averted.

"Well, yes Princess, although I'm sure what we are working on would be best described by Dr. Zeta himself," she replied cordially.

"Oh, so he is here now?" she remarked with an affected surprise. "Why yes, I would love to speak with him. I hope it is no bother."

"No bother at all. I already spoke with him that we might need him for a short exposition. He was happy to do it." She leaned over to one of the attendants. "Please go let Dr. Zeta know that we need him now," she said with a pinched smile. The attendant hurried away.

They sat for a bit, awkwardly waiting for Constant to arrive, all doing their best to be cordial and exchange the proper pleasantries. They tried to fill her in on the news of their life there, while purposefully excluding the attack of the marauders and the events following—they did not want her help on this point in particular, which would most likely come in the form of more armed soldiers.

Finally, the attendant returned with Constant, who had come alone and conspicuously without Owvi. He greeted the Princess as warmly as an old friend and quickly got to his discourse on the generator. He passionately told her of his vision, step by step, beat by beat, and eloquently explained he and Owvi's design for what he had begun to call the "Terrestrial Energy Field Antenna."

As he went, Dr. Whitney found herself slightly irritated at his chummy manner with the Princess and began to have feelings of suspicion towards him. She did not trust the Princess and did not trust anyone who did. She did, however, note that he passed over the central coupling superficially and had also excluded its place into his original vision. She wondered if he had done it purposely. All the same, his exposition was quite moving and otherwise complete.

Perhaps it was his passion for what he called their "chance for technological harmony with the planet of Egolsia," or perhaps it was that he appeared carried away with his explanations, but he seemed much more charming than she had ever seen him before. And when he finished and Princess Fatima took him aside to question him, and laughed loudly at something he said, throwing her head back and touching his arm, a flash of hot rage rang through Dr. Whitey's body.

This surprised her. She was conscious of her dislike for Princess Fatima, as well as her distrust for her—even more so than she let on to the others—and she was also aware that she had experienced certain moments of attraction to Constant, but she had not plumbed the depth of either emotion until she had felt them clash in this way. Still, she was uncertain which of her unconscious feelings had inspired such a reaction. Perhaps both?

Her attraction to Constant seemed logical. He was quite handsome, like some shock white Scandinavian giant. He was obviously intelligent, probably evolved to a degree she couldn't even comprehend. He could be disarming, albeit often aloof. And she had an affection for him as a scientific mind, as a colleague. Yet, she had met him under those types of circumstances that render the sexuality of the opposite person sociologically neutral, often because of the nature of the meeting. And so, when she did experience sensations of attraction, they often came out of nowhere, and at times were quite powerful.

She mused over all this as the meeting finally came to an end. Constant left quickly without speaking to anyone else. Frank had arranged a tour for the Princess, and they left shortly after. Dr. Whitney stayed behind, tending the fire, and wrestling with her thoughts.

* * *

The next morning, while Dr. Whitney took her breakfast in her quarters, a messenger arrived at her door. The Princess had requested for her to come see her privately before she departed. The messenger waited while she finished her meal, then took her to the Princess's airship where she and her detail had passed the night.

Despite her discomfort with having to meet with her again, Dr. Whitney had to admit that she was curious to see the inside of the Princess's airship. The ship appeared to be, by both design and in the way it apparently operated, some sort of blend of terrestrial and probably embargoed off-world technology, that her wealth and access had provided for her. There was also no doubt that there would be some impressive opulence aboard. She was not disappointed.

The ship appeared much larger from within. As soon as they entered, she was conducted down a center hall. It was quite voluminous, so much so that it was almost large enough to be a ballroom, but it was still relatively sparse in its contents. Mainly it seemed to be the nexus for several dozen doors and passageways, spanning three levels. They made their way to a back corridor, with a large nondescript white door. She was told that she was about to enter the Princess's personal quarters.

The space was smaller than she imagined, especially in comparison to the large hall they had come down, but nonetheless impressive. She was led into the living area where she took a seat and was instructed to wait for the Princess. The entire room was encased in what looked like white enamel, which gave off a soft white luminescence. The ceilings were quite tall and soared up to what was probably the underside of the hull, which gracefully curved back to the opposite wall. It was richly but sparsely decorated with an elegant display of tribal art.

A portion of the wall slid open, and Princess Fatima appeared. Dr. Whitney almost didn't recognize her at first. She wore only a long, white, sheer silk gown. She wore no headdress, revealing her completely shorn head. Without her customary pomp and costume, she appeared almost bare before her. Dr. Whitney straightened uncomfortably in her seat.

"Good morning Dr. Whitney" she cooed warmly. "I know you are as busy as I am. Would you like anything to drink?" she said, reaching for a button on the wall.

"No, I'm fine." Dr. Whitney answered back flatly.

"Very well." She smiled and strode over to her with a graceful and unhurried gate. As she moved, the sheerness of her gown became quite apparent—the deep ebony form of her nude body flickered in and out of sight beneath it.

She sat down on the other end of the sofa facing her, and she unconsciously shifted back. A flash of heat went through her body. The impression of the Princess's figure was quite piercing: the severity of her naked head, the deep shine of her brown skin, the contour of her bare breasts traced against the silk of her dress created an attractive but unsettling image. She felt as if she was being let in on something, but she did not yet know what.

"It was no problem at all Princess. Is there something in particular you wished to discuss?" Dr. Whitney prompted her politely, clearing her throat.

The Princess simply smiled and looked at her, for what seemed like too long. She appeared completely relaxed as if they could just sit there in silence, and she would be content for as long as she pleased. Finally, she spoke.

"You know we could be friends, you and I," she said without taking her eyes off her or losing her impossibly warm smile. "We have much more in common than you think."

Dr. Whitney cordially smiled back, without reply.

"I know you don't like me," the Princess continued, clearly not offended by the notion. "And I expect I know why. It is hard for women like us to get along with each other—"

"And what kind of woman is that?" Dr. Whitney quickly broke in.

"Leaders," the Princess replied without skipping a beat. "And I imagine you think I am a privileged being. Handed everything, even genetics," she uncrossed and recrossed her long slender legs, "groomed and grown in some golden hothouse, to rule over others."

"I don't presume to know you, Princess," Dr. Whitney replied coolly. "But, with all due respect, I do find it hard to imagine we've had any kind of similar experience in life." She sat back, placing her hands behind her head, and let out an unconscious sigh. "I think I'll take that drink now."

The Princess smiled, raising an eyebrow. "Coffee? Water?"

"Do you have Whiskey? It's been a while," she replied, making herself more comfortable.

The Princess's eyes flashed with pleasure. "We do." She strode back over to the button on the wall and pressed it. "Two bourbons please," she said speaking to someone hidden behind the elegant wall.

"Right away your Highness," the robotic voice replied.

The Princess returned to the couch, sitting closer to her

this time. She placed her hand familiarly on the back of Dr. Whitney's hand. "I knew we were going to be friends."

Dr. Whitney stiffened again and stared straight ahead. "I wouldn't be too sure," she said with a wry smile but did not take her hand away.

Before Princess Fatima could respond, a low, pleasant tone rang through the room. The libations had arrived in what seemed like an unbelievably short amount of time. Without looking, the princess waved her hand, and the door slid silently open. An attendant, dressed in fatigues, backed into the room, pulling a small brass antique drink cart. The glasses clinked and rattled awkwardly through the silence of the room as the attendant pushed the cart into place before the pair. He quietly poured the brown liquid into two large crystal tumblers and placed a second glass next to each with only large cubes of ice in it. His movements were quick and deft, practiced with the care of an artist, which clashed strangely with his aggressive military attire. He did not look up once.

"That will be all," the Princess informed him. He nodded, again without looking directly at her, and walked to the door. He turned and saluted, before exiting as quickly as he had appeared.

Dr. Whitney picked up her glass, marveling at its large intricately cut cubes of ice, which cracked in the temperature controlled air. It occurred to her that it had been quite a long time since she has seen ice used in a drink, much longer even than she had last tasted whiskey.

"So tell me, Princess, what is it that you want?" Dr. Whitney asked, now turning to look the Princess directly in the eyes.

The Princess again smiled her ineffable smile, unfazed by Dr. Whitney's demand.

"Right to the point. I knew I liked you, Dr. Whitney. Or—may I call you—Sarah? I prefer first name basis. Mine is Atinuke," she said softly, placing her hand back on Dr. Whitney's. "Fatima is actually my second name and the one I use formally. Please don't be surprised that I know your given name, Sarah. Of course, I know all about you, as I'm sure you can imagine I could—I know of your mixed and humble beginnings—your father the activist, your brother the banker… Please sit down."

Dr. Whitney had risen, unsure if she intended to leave, or was just completely taken off guard.

"Please sit," she rejoined, with a sternness that had not been present before. It was the voice of someone that was used to having their way, a voice that was difficult to resist.

Dr. Whitney hesitated, unsure of where this was going. Uncertain of what else to do, she slowly sat back down, and the Princess continued.

"Dr. Whitney, Sarah, of course, I have looked into all the members of the council. I am, as you know, backing something fairly unorthodox here, and I should need to know everything I can about those I am entrusting with my reputation. It is after all my cache in the circles where one can get things such as this done," she said gesturing around her, ostensibly indicated the camp in which the ship now sat.

"Now, as I was saying, I know all about where you come from, and why you choose to go by your middle name, and why you would not trust someone such as myself. But, I want you to trust me, I want you to know me, and to see that we share a common nature, a common interest, if you will," she said, gesturing to her.

"And what interest is that?" Dr. Whitney fired blindly.

The Princess smiled her smile. "We wish the world to bend to give us that which we desire."

Dr. Whitney bristled at the notion. "This is where you are wrong Princess. I do not wish for anyone to bend for me. I only want to ensure a future for us—take back a future that was stolen from us."

"As do I, my dear, as do I. We differ only on perhaps... the details." She moved her hand now to Dr. Whitney's knee. "Listen. There is nothing wrong with such desires my dear. They are natural to women like us. You have the spirit of leader you know, like your father—only, he was misguided. He believed he understood the needs of the people—he did not know that to truly understand them, you cannot be one of them. You see, I simply wish to help you, Sarah. I want to guide you. I want for both of us to get what we want."

"And what is it you want?" Dr. Whitney asked, half incredulously, half in earnest.

"I want to be informed. I want you to keep me in the light on what exactly is happening here. It is very important to me. I don't like being in the dark. When I'm in the dark, I get uncomfortable, and when I'm uncomfortable, it makes it more difficult for me to continue to protect what goes on here. Do you see? It really is such important work—I really don't want for anything to get in the way of it."

Dr. Whitney was now seething internally. As hot as she was, she was still shrewd—it was no accident she had gotten to be where she was. She swallowed and relaxed her hands, which had unconsciously become clenched into hot fists.

"Of course Princess. I shall do my best to keep you comfortable," giving her a pinched smile.

"Good," the Princess replied, taking her hand back. "That will be all then." She stood up quickly. "I look forward to hearing from you. The porter will see you out." And in a sweeping flash of silk, she disappeared through the door from which she had come.

Hardly a beat passed before the fatigue-clad attendant reappeared, ready to escort Dr. Whitney to the exit.

"This is not good," she remarked under her breath as she followed him out.

Chapter 17

Something to be learned

As she trudged back to her house through the snow, Dr. Whitney watched the sleek, awkward shape of the Princess's ship slowly rise, casting a shadow over the camp, and quietly disappear into the mist. It was a relief to watch her go, but the sight of it still gave her chills.

Once snugly back in her quarters, she made tea and retired to her living area to gather her thoughts. She decided not to discuss her conversation with the Princess with Frank and Ambassador Able. At least not yet. It was still not clear to her exactly what sort of Machiavellian intrigue the Princess was up to, and so, for now, she would keep it to herself.

Princess Fatima had been right, she did not trust her. It was true that in the past the Princess had been quite helpful to them. She was quite active in the community of scientists and politicians that worked with and liaised with the local stellar representatives to try to better the deteriorating conditions of their world. So, in many ways, she had no right to be suspicious of her—but she could not shake, nor definitely describe her mistrust for her. Whether it was her gut or simply some sort of prejudice of the ultra-wealthy that she had picked up from her father, she honestly could not tell. All the same, it persisted, and it was hard for her to separate the Princess from the caste from which she came.

The Princess was a member of an extremely wealthy family; a nobility characterized by a long history of well-placed money and political influence. The nobility to which they actually belonged had long since given way to more modern forms of government, though their wealth and access had remained. Her family's position was not so clearly delineated, however. It was true that they were part of one of the most privileged circles of society, but were only adjacent to the sphere of real power possessors— the small number of families that now nearly owned the majority of the wealth of the entire planet, and the handful of mega-corporations that circled about them.

So, the Princess and her family had a great deal of access, and as such, they sat between two worlds. The artifact of her name, and the considerable-but-not-nearly-close-enough wealth of her family, did in fact allow them to enjoy a great deal of influence, though ironically if she had been a member of that truly elite society, she would not have been trusted by the scientists and activists of the philanthropic circle that she also so easily moved through.

It really didn't surprise Dr. Whitney that the Princess had investigated her. It had only really caught her off guard the way in which she had wielded that information, especially the mention her father and her brother. Was it some sort of power play, or possibly some veiled threat, or was she genuinely trying to relate to her in some socially awkward, affluently misguided way?

She cleared her tea and sent for an attendant to help bring hot water for a bath. She needed some time to think, some time to relax.

It had been a long time since she had thought of her father. That was probably because when she thought of him, it always came with the same old mix of emotion—that warmth, anxiety, and sadness that always gave way to a period of questioning what exactly it was she was doing here. Normally, she was a woman that had little time for second guessing herself—she was a woman of action, not contemplation. Her father, however, had been both. "Propping up the corpse of Western Civilization," he would have described her work here.

Her father was a radical. He was a social philosopher and a fierce leader. He had started out the first portion of his adult life as a celebrated professor, who then subsequently dedicated the later part of his life to social and political activism. There was a time where he was the most well known and respected activist leader before he lost the public sympathy by moving to a more radicalized way of thinking, and much more aggressive means of action. She supposed her reaction to this is where she had gotten her more positivist point of view from.

Her father's focus had been on the protection of the people. This had started primarily focused on their rapidly deteriorating environment, and quickly broadened to include the living conditions of all men and woman in their nation. After years of struggle, it ultimately became apparent to him the use of it—the "futility of it all" as he would put it—and he set his sight on the very thing that he believed blocked any hope of progress. He turned exclusively to exposing the dark inner workings of the corporate machine and power elite that according to him stood directly in the way of the betterment of the people.

It was an obviously dangerous road, that slowly led to the stripping away of everything in his life—his reputation, his livelihood, even his family and friends, with the exception of those who fanatically followed him into his losing battle—until one day he disappeared completely. He had knowingly sacrificed himself, and for some unknown reason, that seemed in strange contrast to his later adopted nihilism. On some level, Dr. Whitney still hated him for it, and on another, she deeply respected him.

The attendant had come and filled her bath. As soon as they left, she stripped herself of her gray attire and slid into the hot, waiting water. Tendrils of steam danced off the surface. She closed her eyes.

She had decided to remain at home for the rest of the day, sequestered away from the weather. The snow would be cleared, and melt away. They would begin again when it did—but for today she was not needed. She would spend the rest of the day with her thoughts.

Chapter 18

Construction begins

Owvi looked out from his morning sunlit window. The snow had warmed and then melted away under the swift desert sun as abruptly as it had appeared. Thin layers of white dust that had once shone blue and white, now flashed and puddled into the arid scrub. This captured the attention of Owvi, who had never seen such hectic shifts of nature before. He had experienced hundreds, perhaps thousands, of planetary atmospheres in his day, but never sat within the confines of such hot and cold temporal flashes. To him, it was more than just a curiosity, it was a moment but to observe the delicate balance of an organic system at the moment of collapse.

Construction had begun on the generator. The project had quickly picked up momentum as soon as the camp had been cleared of the unexpected snow. Parties had been organized on resource expeditions to obtain materials, such as the iron and copper that was needed, and had set out on the forbidding plains to either locate scrap sources or abandoned mines where they could be extracted.

Another group had been sent to a nearby quarry to obtain the large raw blocks from which they would painstakingly hew the monoliths. Owvi had given them specific instructions on how to retrieve the blocks, and even how to transport them back to the camp—even though they had modern equipment, it was essential to get it back to camp in a repeatable fashion. It had become clear to them earlier on in the design process that if this was to be a truly lasting and reproducible means by which energy could be generated, then the entire process of construction—including the sourcing of materials and the building process itself—was just as important a part of its fundamental makeup, as were its by-products and the type of energy it output.

With the resource crews well underway on their respective tasks, Owvi had now turned his attention to organizing the construction of the generator. As they moved into the actual creation, Constant had withdrawn himself from the position of construction lead and had entrusted Owvi with that responsibility. It was not that Owvi was necessarily more qualified, it was that Constant was preoccupied and was quite happy being prescribed tasks to complete, so as not to interrupt the process of whatever it was that he was meditating on.

Since the snow had cleared, Constant had taken to the practice of spending more and more of his nights in the desert. After their work was complete for the day, he would take a horse and ride out onto the plains and not come back until the morning. Owvi sensed that he was searching out there for something. Something to help him understand what he was doing here.

He had been quite aware of Constant's inner conflict throughout their time on Egolsia, and especially since their arrival at the community. It was well established between them that what they were doing was highly unorthodox. Owvi was much less concerned about this than Constant. He had no idealized theory to prove, or academic community he was beholden to. He knew Constant was apprehensive about the proof of his theory, and so Owvi was far more interested in the expedition's success based purely on that, than whether what they were doing led to the vindication of some notion or not. Moreover, he did not care how it reflected on him: Owvi simply did not think that way.

Along with their natural inclination toward empathy and their brilliance in engineering, Owvi's people—the Wvio's— were also known for their individualistic, or even described at times as anarchist, mindset toward widely accepted civilized and scientific precepts. They were occasionally reproached by the intergalactic society, to which Constant's people belonged, for their meddling in some affairs that scientific or religious protocol frowned upon, or for their resistance to getting involved in some matters which the larger galactic community believed they should stand together on. This was not to say that they were not a reverent people; they were. It was only that they did not give much thought to other's convention, or even their own, and simply followed their hearts, even if it meant they might end up sometimes in the wrong.

And so, Owvi's primary intention in this mission was not so much his interest in proving Constant's theory on

Contact one way or another, but in helping a friend, for whom he had a great deal of respect and affection, realize his vision. He had no attachment to its outcome, only that it mattered to his friend, and so would do anything in his power to see it through. Whether they ended up chastised or celebrated, it was all the same to him.

And now he had another reason—Tii. He was profoundly captivated by her. And they were both genuinely interested in seeing the generator built and fully functional. And so, this work with her now became the center of his world, as they strained to complete the endeavor in the shortest time possible. For them, time was of the essence.

Chapter 19

Intergalactic love

Owvi stood over the edge of the deep excavation, staring down into the darkness, into the white, luminous face of Tii, who was gazing back at him from below. He adjusted the tout wire that stretched between them ever so slightly and confirmed its new position with his subterranean partner. She gestured her response—they were aligned. Tii smiled up at him.

Owvi took a deep a breath and let out an elated sigh. He was happy. Their work together was flourishing, and so was the bond between them. Though they labored together on quite often mentally and physically demanding undertakings—which regularly required long and intense periods of concentration and lack of sleep—their experience with each other was underlined and punctuated by many moments of joy, where they caught each other's eye and could not help betraying their delight. In a word, they were falling in love.

Currently they were focused on digging a hole. A very deep, and very precise one, but a hole nonetheless. It was the shaft that would receive the monoliths for the underground stage of the generator, and carving out the clay soil to the degree of tolerance that they needed was challenging. They were again confronted with the task of designing a process that was re-creatable without the need for extremely expensive or hard to obtain equipment. A camp engineer had been assigned the job of simply recording their method, which was proving to him to be more of a difficult undertaking than it had sounded.

Owvi and Tii had developed a shorthand between themselves. Sometimes they didn't even speak, a luxury Owvi had ultimately allowed himself with Tii, not so much with her permission, but rather at her insistence. This caused much frustration with the engineer, who was now almost constantly having to interject with questions of what exactly they were doing and saying to each other.

Tii, out of her respect and adoration for Owvi, had in effect become his student. Conversely, from Owvi's perspective, Tii had become his teacher. And so, they had both become for each other an unorthodox student and teacher, master and follower. For each of them respectively, however, this manifested in much different ways. Tii was beginning to learn of the vast knowledge of the universe, and though Owvi was on many levels much more evolved than her, she was growing quickly and had even begun to be able to answer him without speaking, leading to fully silent conversations.

As for Owvi's part, he had never been in love before, at least not like this. This love for her had become the greatest type of teacher for him. He had surely had profound connections with other beings before, but they were not of this amorous kind, not of this chemical and psychological nature. His friendships had been more like the one he had with Constant, or more familial ones, or ones of a more pure mental or intellectual nature.

This was not uncommon for beings of his kind. Owvi's tribe saw eroticism and coupling as not mutually inclusive, and their emotional life and interpersonal social conventions allowed for a multitude of emotional bonds of a variety of types of love. They did create bonds for the purposes of procreation but did not expect or require eroticism to be a part of it. This did not mean they did not have intercourse as a part of normal daily life, only it was often a psychic one—they could have mental intercourse without actually having to be physical. He had shown Tii this on one of the first nights she had stayed with him. She had not left his side since.

Tii nimbly climbed up out of the hole and sprung onto the platform where Owvi stood. She rechecked their measurements—they were not exactly plumb. They would have to re-hone the wall again. She sighed and showed Owvi her calculations.

As the two of them shot back and forth a series of shorthand terms and hand gestures, the engineer tasked with recording them struggled to keep up with the translation. At the end of their brief conversation, Tii nodded and quickly ran off to retrieve something. The engineer looked to Owvi bewildered. He smiled and sat down, gesturing for him to follow. He explained Tii had gone to get some more hands, they had to redo a few things, it was a process. They definitely had some more work to do, and it was going to be a while.

Chapter 20

A view from
another world

The work that day went on into the early evening when
finally they decided to stop for the night. The rest of the
crew shuffled inside in hopes of getting a still warm dinner,
but neither Tii nor Owvi were hungry. They were still abuzz
with the energy they had gained from the efforts they had
made that day, and decide to go lie out on the edge of the
camp and watch the arriving stars.

Tii led him into a fallow garden adjacent to the quarters where Constant was staying. She explained to Owvi
that it was an old rose garden as he had noted the dried
thorns when they entered the low light of its open interior. Constant had already left for the evening to go on his
nightly trip into the desert, leaving the house dark, and
from their position on the hillside, they could barely see
the lights from the camp, and so were able to have a full
view of the darkening sky.

There were clouds passing low on the horizon, catching the last rays of light, which painted them vivid hues of violet and yellow. The cloud cover broke open towards the center of the sky, which was now slowly fading from deep blue to the eternal black and star-speckled dome of the cosmos. The air breathed and a pleasant chill passed over them as they lay down in the damp grass and took in the sight.

They lay there a while, not speaking, quietly watching the stars becoming clearer and clearer, brighter and brighter. Tii could not help herself, and leaned over and asked Owvi to point out his home if he could. He began to try and explain gravitational curvatures and the misleading artifact of distant light, but soon abandoned it at the sight of her wide smiling eyes, and simply pointed to a bright cluster a short distance from the center of the sky and said "there." She smiled at him in appreciation.

A songbird pierced the quiet evening air. Tii sat up to try and find it in the low light. It fluttered its feathers as it sang its song again, and they were able to catch sight of it as the branch it was sitting on flickered in the bush. It was twilight, but they still could see its beautiful blue color. It called out again.

"It's so beautiful," Tii said turning to Owvi. "I wonder what the stars look like through his eyes?"

Owvi paused for a moment, considering, then placed his hand gently on hers.

She immediately felt a strange falling sensation and involuntarily closed her now drowsy eyes. Suddenly she felt her heart break into what felt like a thousand pulsing heartbeats, beating faster than she could have imagined.

Her eyes shot back open, and she saw the lights of the stars swirling above her, shadows flashed one moment abstractly, another moment crystal clear. Her appendages flailed about in chaos, and she felt as though she was sinking again, but then in the next moment she was floating steadily, and then even rising into the air.

It was a sensation she had never felt before, perhaps but in her dreams. The horizon finally stabilized and came into focus, and the chaos and initial terror seemed to fade away. She could feel her will to rise manifest with the pressure she was able to exert on the air around her. For a moment, she was free. She was flying.

Her view turned back down toward Earth, and she could see Owvi beneath her, smiling back up at her. Next to him was another figure, which she quickly recognized as herself. This sight confused her, and she immediately began to fall. The darkness swallowed her as she fell into bewilderment, all the way down…

She woke moments later, opened her eyes slowly and looked around. Owvi sat across from her smiling, stroking a slightly dazed bird which he now held cupped in his hand. Seeing her, it jumped up and flew away at once.

"Did that really just happen?" she asked half laughing, still a little confused. Owvi was now stroking her hair, as he had been with the little bird.

"We all see the same light—the eyes are only tuned to slightly different frequencies. They all peer through slightly different sides of the same prism. There is only one source you know," he answered cryptically, then laughed.

She laid back down, content now not to question her

experience. They sat for a while in silence again, in wordless admiration of the starry sky, and spent the night quietly discussing other worlds, and exchanging ideas that few on her planet had ever conceived of.

Chapter 21

Stantish returns

The following afternoon, a small commotion arose at the gate, breaking the contemplative rhythm of the ongoing construction. Those who were not immediately engaged wove their way down through the piles of building materials to discover what exactly the commotion was about: Stantish had returned. Storm was not with him.

He stood in the middle of an impatient group, who were eager to understand what had transpired, peppering him with: "Where are the bandits? Where is Storm? Were they coming back? Were they dead? Where had they gone?" all which made for the majority of the questions. He seemed unable to reply, shedding his gear where he stood. Someone with some sense appeared with water for him to drink.

It had been quite a while since he had departed camp with Storm, pursuing the bandits into the desert, intent on making sure they would not return. He was now covered in a film made of the desert floor—dusted down, drab and beige, caked with deep red blood stains on his skin and clothes, as if the sand were making a desperate attempt to soak up the horror and make it disappear. His eyes were wild—caged—as they trained towards Constant. They were clear with meaning. Constant motioned Stantish toward him, away from the group. Dr. Whitney understood their meaning too and made sure the crowd did not follow.

Stantish started to speak, but Constant motioned for him not to. He took him by the arm and guided them further down the path. They could see Frank coming down the same direction to join them. Constant turned and asked Stantish with his characteristically matter-of-fact tone, "So?"

"We killed them," he replied, without a beat. He looked at Constant, then away, then back at him, obviously apprehensive of his response, and with no desire to talk about it.

Constant did not reply. He only returned his gaze. After an awkward pause, seeing Constant was not going to be the one to speak, he took a seat by the path, and began his report all the same. Frank ran up breathlessly just as he began—he too wanted a report on their pursuit, which Stantish now hotly gave to the both of them.

And so, there he sat, unfolding all of the events that had transpired, starting with the very day they had left, to how they had arrived at that very, unexpectedly violent terminus. And why Storm was not with him.

Stantish and Storm had set out south across the Grand Mile, heading to its southwesternmost border. They had taken the military transport that Stantish had driven them all in from the underground base in the south, and because of its speed, there were able to catch a warm trail. They were immediately confident that were they on the right path, and that they would catch up with their now fleeing assailants soon enough. As they reached the southernmost ridge, however, they realized their mission would not be so simple, or so easy.

They had scrambled their transport to the top of the ridge and stopped there. Below, on the far side, they saw several abandoned vehicles—undoubtedly some of the same ones they had been chasing. The vehicles were all blackened and charred, no doubt having been set fire to by their occupants as they fled, in an attempt to cover their tracks and prevent anyone from using them to pursue them. They got out of their vehicles and made their way tentatively down the ridge to inspect the still smoking craft, some of them with their doors still open, scorched safety belts swinging uselessly.

A knot-work of tire tracks surrounding the wrecks told the story. They had abandoned their vehicles most likely for faster, or perhaps simply fully functioning ones, as many of them had taken heavy fire during the siege. Or maybe this was their exit strategy all along, not wishing to risk all of their transportation, and ensuring themselves an exit, they had executed their plan to its last detail. Either way, they were gone, with only these burned hulls left as a trace.

Storm climbed atop one of the now useless machines and took out his field glass. He scanned the horizon for any sign of the escaping bandits. There was none. He exchanged glances with Stantish, who was still inspecting the tracks. He nodded. They did this often now—not speak—as there was an understanding between them, and they were often of one mind. The communication had been: they would pursue the fleeing group. They would not let them escape.

They headed off west, through the southernmost pass, occasionally stopping to check for tracks. They were confident they were heading in the right direction, as there was not much of a choice in the course along this passage. They had slowed their pace as they were well aware of the possibility that they were being set up for an ambush, and were now continually scanning the ridge line for any signs of life.

They tracked the bandits like this for several days. The further they went, the farther the pursued ran, and the more deeply set became their resolve. They had become like a predator chasing its prey: the faster the prey ran, the more focused and aggressive the predator became. And moreover, the more convinced they became of the sophistication of the group they were following, the more aware they were of its danger. These were not some wretched scrap of wanderers and thieves, forced into making a desperate plea for their survival by attacking another community. They had a plan, they had a backup plan. This is what they did. This is how they lived their lives.

Occasionally they found a series of still smoldering fires that assured them they were on the right track, but it was unclear if the retreating group knew if they were being followed or not. They moved through the desert with a practiced lightness, leaving very little sign of themselves in their wake, yet they apparently made no attempt to cover some of the campsites that they left behind. Perhaps they were leaving them untouched in order to make their pursuers think they were unaware of them, lulling them to drop their guard. Perhaps this type of exit was a matter of operation for them, whether or not their raid had been successful. These were the types of discussions Storm and Stantish had when they occasionally broke their silence.

On the fifth day of their pursuit, they reached a narrow pass through a high mountain ridge. They cautiously approached, moving stealthily through the cracks and crevasses of the mountain, till they reached the other side. There, down on the valley floor, tucked between the small high plain and the far mountain, was the dark smudge of a nomadic camp.

Chapter 22

From the shadows

Stantish and Storm could not tell from their vantage point whether or not this was the group they were looking for. They had lost the trail they had been following a ways back and had only landed at this spot by following the natural trajectory of their previous path. The group was definitely nomadic by the look of the few hastily erected tents, and moreover, by the encircling of their fortified vehicles, but there was just no telling if this was the same group they were searching for without having a closer look. They decided to find a secure position and camp for the night.

Night came and with it a heavy discussion. What was their plan? If these were actually their attackers, what would they do? They decided the first thing they needed to do was make confirmation that this was, in fact, the group that had attacked them, and then they would decide how to proceed.

All of their options seemed untenable. If it was them, and they went back for reinforcements, it was likely, or at least possible, that the camp would be long gone by the time they returned. If that happened, it would probably be impossible for them to find them again. Until that is, they perhaps showed up one night back at North Camp, this time really taking them by surprise. If they tried to engage them merely in an attempt to scare them off, it was likely it would not go well for them, based solely on their unequal numbers. It could even end up with them drawing the bandits into a reverse pursuit. Still, they had tracked them this far, and they needed to know if it was actually them, even if the end result was merely them returning to the camp to report the bandits had gone on their way.

They decided to sleep on it.

In the morning, they hid their vehicle, scrubbed their camp in case they did not return, and headed down into the valley. Their plan was to get close enough to observe the inhabitants of the camp, and preferably get visual confirmation that these were the bandits they had been tracking.

They both took up different positions in the cascading boulders that bordered the camp. They watched through their field glass, scrutinizing the activities of each of the inhabitants they were able to focus in on. The day was long and hot, and the sun burned their necks, but they kept to their task. So far they had only observed them at work amongst the most trivial of life's daily chores. Their central fire was fed with a cache of wood bars that looked as if they had been streamlined for portability. People were smoking what looked like meat around the fire. Some were attending to the maintenance of their vehicles, and others were simply moving about with obvious but invisible purpose. It wasn't until the sun began to set that they saw anything out of the ordinary.

As the day's activities wound down, they noticed a group of men start to form outside of one of the tents. They were dressed somewhat differently than the other inhabitants, who mostly wore what looked like clothes of the age, albeit much dirtier from the desert. They all seemed preoccupied with some discussion they were having amongst themselves and were energetically gesturing toward the mountains and back toward the tent. Soon, another man came out, immediately capturing the attention of the group.

He too was dressed differently, as the other men were, but even more so. His whole body was tightly wrapped head to toe in what appeared to be dark animal skins. Only his head was unwrapped, atop which sat a dark crop of wild hair, like a lion's main. His visage was disfigured by a long scar which ran the entire diagonal length of his face—visible even within the field glass's limited magnification. Clearly, by the way others moved around him, he was some kind of leader, perhaps the leader of the entire enterprise. They watched carefully.

Another man ran up to them, carrying a large sheet of worn looking paper. They could not make out what it was but assumed it was a map based on how they gestured between it and the mountains. They were pointing in the direction they had come. The leader turned back and went inside, taking a few of the men with him. The others stayed outside and waited, no longer speaking this time.

They watched until dark. The first set of men who had gone in the tent had left, and the others went in, ostensibly to receive their instructions, but the leader never reemerged.

The activity of the camp was now appearing to wind down for the day, so Stantish and Storm decided to go back up the hillside and camp for the night.

They lit a small fire, confident that it could not be seen in the valley below, and sat down to discuss what they had seen. There was little doubt between the two of them that these were the bandits, but also little proof. The clothing the group of men had been wearing seemed similar to the clothing worn by the attackers, but there was no way they could be certain. The vehicles parked around the camp too appeared armored in a similar way as the ones used in the raid, but as they were obviously not the same ones, since those had been destroyed, there was no proof in that either.

It began to dawn on them that there was no easy way for them to prove that these were the people they were tracking. They only had their gut, and their gut told them yes. Perhaps if they were able to sneak into camp and find that map, they could make a reasonable confirmation—if the North Camp was marked on it, then they knew it was too much of a coincidence and would proceed accordingly. They could steal the map too, or sabotage them somehow, or in some way prevent or discourage them from making a second attack on the camp. Either way, they needed to get into that tent.

Without warning, there was a movement in the shadows around the edges of their camp. A figure had moved into the firelight and then turned and ran. Storm was quick to react and immediately chased after him, out into the darkness. The pursuit did not last long, however, and Storm was soon walking back into the firelight, panting, dragging a flailing figure by his collar. He threw him to the ground in front of Stantish.

"Stay!" he commanded him, bending over to momentarily catch his breath.

Stantish stood over the intruder, taking him in. He was a younger man, dressed in a fashion similar to the men they had seen, wrapped intermittently with blacked animal skin and heavy woven dusted cloth. He cowered away from them, shrinking back from the fire.

"Sit up. We're not going to hurt you. What are you doing here?" Stantish asked him, with a deliberately calm voice.

The man sat up, his face illuminated in the firelight. He was quite young, with a filthy face and a sparse but course stubble beard. His hair was long and oily and hung in his face. He pushed it back with his hand.

"Who are you?" he replied defiantly.

Storm appeared from the darkness behind him. He grabbed him by the hair and pressed his knife to his throat. "Answer him."

Stantish winced at Storm's aggression with the boy, but he knew the stakes were getting high here—they needed to know who these people were. The young man stubbornly did not answer.

"Are you the ones who attacked us? Did you run from us here?" Storm demanded.

He looked at the both of them. "I don't even know who you are," he snarled and spat in the dirt.

"Then what are you doing here?" Stantish persisted.

"I'm lookout here. It's my job. Ya see. Lookin' out for people like you," he snorted.

Stantish crouched down. "Then you were looking for us. Why did you attack us? It doesn't look like you're desperate."

The young man looked back at him incredulously and laughed. "Mister, I don't even know who you are, cuz you sure ain't from around here. This here whole land is desperate. We get what we want, how we want. We get what we can, how we can, ya see."

He smiled a half-snarl half-smile of broken teeth, looking up at the two of them standing over him, though his wild, oily locks. He grinned wider.

"Desperate huh?" The young man continued. "You think this land gonna reach up out of thish here dirt and hand us our meal? Huh. We done bit that hand off. This here is what ye call your dog-eat-dog world. And then some. And we just out here trying to get our eat before we get eaten."

Stantish and Storm exchanged glances. "Did you hear what we were talking about?" Stantish asked cautiously. The young man ignored him, laughing to himself.

"Where you boys think you are anyway? This here is Mars, man. This ain't Earth. Not no more. You think them city folk care what we do out here? They can't barely feed themselves, keep from killin' themselves. There ain't no laws out here, man—only our rules, our laws—the laws of this damn desert here, yessir."

"Did you hear what we were talking about?" Stantish insisted, searching his face.

The young man paused and looked him back in the eye. He smiled.

"Yeah," he huffed. "You think your gonna 'saber-tage' us or some such stuff. But I tell you this boy, these here dogs got more bite than bark, and if you think you just gonna come up in our house... our house..." The young man trailed off muttering expletives to himself.

Storm took Stantish aside. "What are we going to do?" he asked him, unsure of what his answer would be.

"We'll have to keep him here until we can decide what to do with him," Stantish replied.

Storm looked back at him, shaking his head.

"The fuck you are—" they heard as the young man abruptly sprang from the ground and knocked over Stantish as he leapt for the darkness. Just as he reached the edge of the light, an awkward protrusion seemed to suddenly shoot out from the back of his head. The man stopped short. He sunk to his knees, as dark red blood flooded out from the angular protuberance, covering his back and running down his thighs. He fell forward onto his face, into the dust, silent. It all seemed so surreal.

Stunned, Stantish turned to find Storm. He was standing there with his arm still extended in the frozen form from which he had thrown his knife. Stantish's gaze finally broke the spell Storm was under. He slowly dropped his hand, still stiff, to his side.

"I couldn't let him leave," Storm said numbly.

Stantish got up and walked over to the fallen man. He was lying face down in the dirt, with a large red-brown stain blooming around his head, pooling in the dusty ground. He could see the flash of the blade in the firelight. The man was not moving, he was not breathing. He was dead.

Stantish suddenly became nauseous. He ran to the edge of camp, and vomited an unexpected amount of beige liquid, as his day's water rations splashed out flatly onto the desert floor. From behind him, he could hear Storm repeating to himself evenly.

"We couldn't let him leave. We couldn't. I don't think I could have caught him that time. He would have gone back and told the others. They would have hunted us down. They would have attacked us again. It was us or him. Listen, it was us or him."

Stantish turned back towards him. "I'm not sure I know the difference anymore."

Chapter 23

Desert on fire

Assuming someone in the camp below would notice the young man's absence when he did not return the following morning, and come looking for him, Stantish and Storm decided to move up their timeline to that very evening. They were now quite convinced that the nomads were, in fact, planning a second attack; they did not have proof, but it is what their gut told them, and told them strongly.

They had considered the possibility of simply returning and notifying the North Camp of the coming assault, giving them time to prepare, but this would be their one chance to take them by surprise, their one chance to stop them from attacking them again. A lot of lives could be lost this time. The camp could be lost. Or worse.

They did their best to bury the body in a shallow grave and again scrubbed the campsite in case they did not return. They retrieved their rifles from their vehicle for protection—only as a precaution Stantish insisted—and made their way down to the valley below. The camp was clearly not guarded. They noted the occupants must obviously believe themselves safe in this refuge before they both realized that was probably the young man's job to stand guard and spot anyone well before they got there.

The plan they had conceived was fairly simple: Storm would disable the vehicles and Stantish would see if he could locate the map. They estimated that with their vehicles impaired, at least temporarily, and along with the added tactical disadvantage of losing the map, they would at least reconsider the second attack, or hopefully even stay away forever. That would be the most ideal scenario.

Storm went first, moving stealthily out toward the ring of vehicles that flanked the camp. His aim was to cut every line and wire that he could get his hands on without creating any noise. Moving from the refuge of the boulders, he disappeared quickly into the black of night. Stantish took a deep breath. He did not like any of this. All the same, he himself now crept quietly into the camp. He wove around the tents, keeping to the shadows, moving with the utmost care. Everyone was obviously asleep as it was quite late, but the last thing he wanted to happen was to run into someone who had come out on the edge of camp to urinate, and start an all-out war.

He made his way through a gauntlet of undesirable shadows, and unexpected sounds, which swelled in the terror of the darkness. With beads of sweat on this forehead, and swallowing his heaving breath as best he could, he finally found the tent where they had seen the men gather earlier that day. His thought was that the tent was some sort of office or command center and that hopefully there was no one sleeping in there. Even if there was, he would hopefully be able to hear them breathing before going in. In that case, he would creep back to the refuge behind the boulders, and the sabotaging of their vehicles would have to suffice for this mission. He gently pulled the flap back and slowly put his head inside, listening.

The tent was nearly black inside, though not completely dark as a small vent at the top was letting some of the moonlight shine in from the night. The blue in his eyes adjusted to the new level of light, as his ears strained and searched the room in all of its crevices. He could hear no sounds. There was no one in the tent. He went in.

As soon as he was inside, he quickly dove to the floor when he felt the first large object impede his ingress—he rolled to the side and sunk under a large table, panting. He could feel the cool of the flattened desert floor under his fingertips, as he waited for his eyes to finish adjusting. Wildly he searched the room, as the full picture of its contents formed in the dim light. The chill of the night's air passed from the open door into the room.

He had been right, it appeared to be some sort of office or central command. There were only a few major pieces of furniture, and those consisted of three large tables that took up most of the room—one under which he now sat. They were filled with what appeared to be various writing tools, papers, wax draped candles, large lumps of shadows, and other indiscernible objects. At the rearmost table, curling over the edges with large white sheets was a pile of paper that seemed like his best place to find the map he believed them to possess. There was no better way that he could think to proceed, so he stood up and calmly walked over to it.

The back of the room was cast more deeply in shadows, but upon reaching the table, he was still to able to barely make out what looked like some sort of contour map. It occurred to him that the map was upside down, so he gingerly lifted it and spun it to face him. He strained at the image in the dark. It was hard to tell, but it appeared the contours did, in fact, represent the local region, the desert, and mountains that surrounded it. He struggled to place anything exactly though. Engrossed, he lifted it to the slashes of moonlight which penetrated the room to see if he could read it any better. The hairs on his neck suddenly stood up. He heard breathing. There was someone in the room with him. He spun around.

There, in front of him, loomed the face of the man that he had seen from a distance earlier that day. White and ghastly in the dull moonlight, a face split by a scar that ran its length, and crowned by tousled black locks. It spoke.

"Who are you?" the face demanded.

"I—" Stantish barely got it out. Without a full beat passing, the man had already removed a knife from his keep and lunged it towards the center of Stantish's chest. Stantish managed to blindly deflect it off center before it plunged hotly into his right shoulder. He shrieked in pain.

The ghostly man immediately withdrew the knife for a second strike. Reacting strictly from the muscular memory of one who had studied the ceremonial art of war without ever a true thought to its reality, Stantish's first hand grappled the knife as the second followed, driving it up with the heel of his palm into the soft underside of the chin of the unknown man, all the way up to the hilt. Blood flowed down Stantish's wrist, warm and wet. The man spat bloody fluid from his mouth, staring back at him with still lit eyes.

The life that continued to flicker in them made clear that the tip of the blade had missed its mark. Instead of cleanly cleaving the frontal lobe, the blade had pierced the roof of his mouth and most likely tore through his sinuses—

The man gasped, spitting up more blood, and strained to speak with his failing breath.

"We're not your enemy," he whispered.

Stantish, still in shock, humanly rotated the knife, penetrating the brain, and the ghost left the man's body. His now empty vessel sank to the floor. Trembling uncontrollably, Stantish dropped the knife, but still stood frozen from the shock of it all. He had never killed another human being before. Nor had he killed any being of a higher brain order for that matter—not on his home planet, and certainly not on one where he was a guest. Even though his culture meticulously simulated it in the retelling of their ancestor's past, and even though they ceremoniously trained their young with the real ability to do it, he, and really no one in his society, ever expected to actually perform the act: to kill. They had previously seen killing as a necessity, and then subsequently, a very much unnecessary stage in their evolution, and now the act was just not done. In fact, it was reverently abhorred.

A shot rang out somewhere in the camp, snapping Stantish out of his stupor. Someone must have spotted Storm. He knelt down and picked up the wet knife. Disgusted, he let it drop back to the floor and slipped quietly out of the tent.

He could see flashes of rifle fire through a newly formed cloud of smoke and dust on the other side of the camp. There was no one around him at the moment, but if this man he had just so tragically laid low was, in fact, their leader, then someone would be coming for him soon. He crept back around the back of the tent and made a sudden run for the black border of night. He quickly made his way through the maze of brush out into the dark of the plateau. From a distance he could see the battle more clearly; Storm was pinned down behind the boulders, locked in a firefight. Taking a deep breath, he headed directly for him, delicately skirting the edge of the darkness.

He was able to move up to Storm's position so stealthily that when he finally did reach him, Storm quickly spun around, wild-eyed, and aimed his rifle directly at Stantish's head. Seeing it was him, he turned back to the fight, brusquely telling him to get his rifle out. Stantish reluctantly complied, but he certainly did not plan on using it.

"Fire at them!" Storm shouted.

"No," he replied weakly.

"If you don't we will both be dead," Storm shouted back, still firing.

Stantish peered through a crack. He saw two dark bodies strewn not far in front of the boulder. It was clear they had made a rush for it, and Storm had stopped them short. Beyond them, he could see the periodic flashes of rifle fire from behind a few of the nearby vehicles. It was possible they were pinned down too and had dug in. A small fire had started behind them.

Another set of cracks and flashes came from somewhere around the corner of one of the tents. Storm pressed himself against the rock but did not return fire. He was counting on the ones behind the vehicles to eventually make a run for it. He was right.

As soon as the two shadows fled out, Storm popped back up, shouting to Stantish, "Give me cover fire!" and began firing heavily at them. He caught one of the fleeing figures in the heel, who yelped in pain as he slid headlong into the dust. Stantish leveled his gun and watched for a flash from the other gunman. It came. The sand popped angrily near Storm's feet, and the rock that shielded them zinged and spat, but he did not stop firing. Stantish did not want to kill anyone else, but he knew he had to shoot back if only to keep Storm from being gunned down. He aimed at what he estimated was well above their head height and fired back.

Another fire had started on one of the vehicles, and the original one had now grown considerably. They were whipping and heaving in the fierce desert wind and looked as if they were about to lose control.

The firing momentarily stopped from the other side, and they could hear what sounded like a panic coming from within the encampment. Shadows flashed and flickered in the growing light. Stantish and Storm briefly discussed making a run for it, up into the hills to ultimately try and make it to their vehicle. They decided against it. They now held the best cover between where they were and where their vehicle was, and if they were caught out in the open, or cornered on the foothills, they would most likely not survive. They would stand their ground and wait until they were sure they could make a move.

They turned their attention back to the camp. The fire had spread to the tents. There was still a commotion going on, but they could not hear exactly what it was. Suddenly five figures emerged from the shadows of the camp and steadily walked towards them. The figures opened fire.

The boulder popped and hissed under the violence of the gunfire. Stantish and Storm remained pressed with their backs against the rock, sweating and panting, trying to control their breath. The gunmen continued to advance. Finally, Storm turned to Stantish and said, "I'm sorry." Without another word, and before Stantish could stop him, he moved out from behind the great rock and started firing.

The surface of his clothing immediately began to convulse with the spray of bullets that were passing through it. It did not deter him. He continued to fire back in kind, striking each of the other figures several times over. Three dropped immediately from wounds to their heads. The other two continued to move forward towards Storm, as he moved towards them, the three exchanging fire, and taking it until at last they nearly met, and all three fell forward onto the ground, their lifeblood finally running out of their bodies onto the dry desert floor. It was suddenly quiet.

Stantish could not move. He could hear screams now coming from the camp, and the roar of the fire that now raged uncontrollably. He held his back against the cold rock and prayed to his God that another being would not come towards him. He could not raise his hand again. He could stomach no more death.

Desert on fire

There he sat, mechanically listening to the terrifying sounds coming from the camp, and wept. Slowly as the night faded and the Sun started to rise, the sounds became quieter and quieter until at last there were no sounds at all.

* * *

It was nearly mid-morning before Stantish finally moved, peeling himself away from the face of the boulder. He looked out from behind the rock. It was quiet. Carefully, he pulled himself along the desert floor to Storm's body, which lay indiscriminately amongst the dead.

There was something morbidly intimate about the scene; the brutalized men lying there together, all stained with the same red, their blood mingled together, quiet, like brothers. Stantish pressed his face against Storm's already cooling one and wept. He was his brother. And now he was gone. It was an honorable death, and he prayed over his body to the Great Spirit of War. He would be remembered.

Turning his attention to the still smoking encampment, he cautiously made his way into the smoldering ruin. A great deal had burned. There were not bodies everywhere, as he had feared, but that did not take the sting away when he finally did see them. Some were burned beyond recognition, others only partially so, but for the most part it was unclear if those who lain amongst the ashes had died by gunshot first, or had been simply burned alive.

As he reached the center of the encampment, he noticed a curious scene. There did appear to be some evidence that the camp's inhabitants had, in fact, attempted to put out the fire, though obviously unsuccessfully, with slapdash buckets of water that now lay impotently in the blackened dust. Near to them lay a few figures, that appeared to have died by stab wounds, and based on the circumstances, either by each other's hands or by some of the other inhabitants. Perhaps there was some sort of mutiny—perhaps one group want to stay and fight or protect the camp, and the other, not knowing how many were with Stantish and Storm, wanted to flee.

He made his way over to the far edge of the camp to look for evidence of this exodus. He found it—or so he could best surmise. There was a trail of footprints and drag marks heading out of the North edge of camp, out into the desolate land beyond. He squinted at the horizon but saw nothing. They were probably quite far away at this point. It was impossible for him to tell exactly how many of them there were, but he wished it was as many as possible. This had all been a terrible mistake.

He found his way back towards the tent that he had searched the night before. It only now occurred to him that he had never taken the map he had gone there for in the first place; the very thing that had put him in a position to kill. He would get it now. It had to mean something.

As he walked up, he noticed the tent was partially burned, and moreover, there was a charred body lying at the mouth of it. He went straight to it, picking up the macabre black figure in his arms. He stared into its charred face, its lipless, bare toothed smile seemingly grinning back at him. Though burned, he saw the wound under its chin. It was him. Someone had no doubt tried to drag the body from the tent, only to abandon him to the raging fire. He held him in his arms, remembering what he had said as he died: "We are not your enemy."

Chapter 24

The test

Three weeks after Stantish's return, and after a considerable amount of effort and concentration from all involved, they were now finally preparing the generator—or Terrestrial Energy Field Antenna, as Constant liked to call it—for testing. Stantish, in a most dejected state, had thrown himself thoroughly into the process of construction, joining Constant and his team members in the quiet meditation of building this singular structure. At this point, nearly everyone else in the camp had also joined the group in the task. For engineers and builders, Tii had been the point person, passing on all the instructions and understanding that she was receiving from Owvi to anyone who was able to receive it. The camp had become an oddly quiet place, save for the sounds of tools on materials, the occasional spoken direction, and other such contemplative sounds of focused work.

The resource team leaders had returned just a few days after Stantish, each with positive news, either bringing back the necessary materials themselves or a clear plan on their retrieval. This was the first success of the project, as it at least proved the part of the theory that demanded that the materials be relatively easy to source or easy to find.

One of the most challenging parts of the project turned out to be the metalworking and casting process. The metal shop had been expanded, and a new oven had been designed and built in order to more quickly and efficiently reach the extremely high temperatures that were needed to forge the metals necessary for the composition of the generator. Constant and another engineer were in charge of the casting processes, and Owvi and Tii were in charge of testing the components. It was a long process of calculating, shaping, casting, measuring, testing, recasting, remeasuring, over and over and over again until they got each part right. It was a process where many of the crew did not sleep for several consecutive days, not tiring, not stopping until each piece was fashioned to the highest possible tolerance.

In the meantime, Stantish and his crew had constructed a scaffolding from which the generator, and then its respective housing, would be assembled. The housing was one part weatherproofing and one part camouflage so that at a distance, it would appear to the casual observer as something like a farmer's storage silo.

When all pieces were complete, the entire community came out to help in its final assembly. It was an exciting but quite trepidatious time. They were all obviously eager to see if the generator would actually work, but moreover many of them had now put all of their hopes into its success. Indeed, whether this thing worked or not could very well determine whether the experiment that was this community was a success or a failure. Few worked without that question on their mind.

Finally, it was complete. Owvi and Tii had triple checked the measurements, and hand spun all of the components—everything checked out perfectly. The enclosure had been mostly finished, with one side left open, so that everyone could clearly see its operation. One of the electricians had set up two posts on either side of the tower and strung dozens of lights between them. He had then hooked them up to the transformer to which the generator was attached. This would allow everyone standing below to nearly instantly see the result of the test: if the lights went on, it was good, if not, there was a problem. They all smiled at it, for it was a somewhat dramatic approach, as a simple voltmeter would have sufficed, but everyone who was now gathering there appreciated a bit of theater for all of their efforts.

Dr. Whitney and Frank were up on the platform with the rest of the core team of builders, who had all squeezed up there to be a part of the test. The rest of the crew was down with the remainder of the community, nervously conversing with each other, each trying their best to temper their anticipation. When Constant and Owvi appeared, carefully carrying the yet to be installed final component, the crowd pressed forward, craning their necks and hushing each other until the din died down.

The generator had been built without an "on" and "off" switch, against the usual Egolsian standards. This was partially to reduce manufacturing needs, but mainly because once this device was set in motion, it was supposed to just keep moving, and only be stopped for the purpose of the maintenance of its components. That is to say, it was much less of what would be locally described as an electrical circuit, and more like a water wheel, except driven by the universal terrestrial energy field instead of simply water.

Constant and Owvi ceremoniously stooped down and slid the central coupling into place. Slowly they stood back as if some shift in the air might disturb the freshly placed part. They knew better, but the excitement of it, the weight of it all, had affected them too. They all waited intently.

Ever so slowly, the components began to turn. Absolute silence fell over the crowd—the slowly winding pieces had captured their complete attention. Some forgot to breathe. Others grabbed the hands of their neighbor. The sections continued to wind about each other, faster and faster. A sort of hum began, a vibration in the soil beneath their feet—it was not the generator making a sound, but the settling of the ground itself. It soon quieted down as the generator picked up speed. There was no sound coming directly from it, as most of its components that could cause friction did not actually touch, but were separated by an infinitesimal magnetic field definitively pushing them apart. The only sound they could hear was the whoosh of air that had been kicked up in the chamber between the housing and the topmost component.

The crowd remained hushed. A few yelps began to penetrate the silence as the telltale metallic clank of the transformer starting up, now putting off its own hum, thrummed through the air. All eyes were now on the lights. And they did not disappoint. One by one the strands flickered on—but the crowd did not move, did not speak—until the last was lit. They all beamed brightly in the new night. The entire community shouted and cried out in unity, the ones who had forgotten to breath were now grasping for air. They embraced each other; some danced to silent songs, some shouted with relief, and some just beamed with delight. It was a success.

The celebration quickly moved into full-scale revelry, as bottles of precious spirits that had been long hidden for such a special occasion, now found their way into the waiting glasses. Everyone was elated. This was not only a success for them but a revolution in engineering that could change the circumstances of their entire people.

Constant too was happy, but he was also tired. He excused himself early from the celebration, quietly slipping back to his quarters, as the slow magic of evening came down upon the camp, now crowned with dozens of new lights.

Chapter 25

Night on the plains

Constant silently packed his small desert kit with the same meticulous ceremony as he had done so many nights before. The success of the day's work hummed in his body and sought to slow him down, but the sun was now setting, and he still wanted to get out on the plain before the light had gone completely. He sped up his work.

His pack was modest—all desert dusted and worn, outfitted with a heavy woven blanket, a canteen, and only a few other essentials—but for him, it had become something of an accoutrement of an almost religious ceremony. He had been spending more and more time out there in the desert, doing what he liked to call "communing." He wrapped himself in an old pelt, pulled a worn, wide brim hat over his brow, and set out for the stable.

His horse too had become part of the ceremony, and moreover, his sacred companion—a partner in the mysterious dance they both had been partaking in—which, step by step, had unfolded to them in the seemingly unfathomable desert, night after night. He hurried through the slowly dimming stable to his horse, who he had aptly renamed Cloudfoot, in honor of his participation. He met him in his stall with a sweet but quiet reverence, speaking softly to him as he fed and prepared him for the night's journey. Having placed a heavy blanket over his back to brace him against the cool night air, they set out through the cultivated fields to the desert beyond.

The sun had begun its descent as they cleared the green fields and trotted down the gentle hillside into the valley flat below. Usually, he would cross to the far west side to a set of hills, atop of which was a large stone outcropping that soared wildly into the sky. He considered that place sacred, and it was there where he had spent most of his nights in communion. Tonight, however, he had decided to explore a path he had noticed that led up into the hills which bordered the northern side of the plain. It was there he now headed.

He turned his horse up the pass as the sun shed its last few rays of the day, compelling the mountains around him into the blue-green hue of twilight. He loved this place, and he loved this moment most of all. It was in this moment that, to him, the desert truly awakened. It was almost, but not completely quiet, as the animals changing guard were still to be heard. It was the Spirit of the Desert that he felt emerge now, the Sun slowly giving its jurisdiction over to it for the night. He felt, though could not see, the hills begin to teem with stirring spirits, and wordless secrets that seemed as ancient as the hills themselves. It was as if there was this old and flourishing life, a world that lay just beyond his sight, on the tip of his tongue to account, but he had not the material makeup to directly perceive it with his physical organs.

The hills opened up and out onto a high plain beyond. He stopped his horse at the peak of the pass and looked out across its vastness. It truly was grand, and the sight of it bent the eye as it tried to grasp its entirety. Somewhere out in its center, he noticed a broad set of white lines thinly streaking up from the desert floor. Curious, he set down the pass on his horse at a faster pace than he usually wished to demand from him, so that he would be able to get a better look at this anomaly before the plateau descended into complete darkness.

As he drew closer, what loomed before him bore an eerie resemblance to some sort of graveyard of strange giant beings. There were rows upon rows of massively tall, spindly, and what appeared to be metal towers, with equally massive petal-like blades atop them. There were hundreds of them, perhaps even thousands, organized in a large repetitive geometric grid. He quickly came to understood what they were, but the impression did not leave. It was a dead wind farm.

He craned his neck as he slowly led his horse through the stark white rows, which were now washed by the last purple glow of twilight. A few of the blades still moved, though heavily grinding against whatever rust had put a stop to the others. Most of them were frozen in place or hanging broken like the wilted petals of a dying flower. It truly was a graveyard. Only, instead of the foot of each structure marking buried remains below, they only symbolized the petrified death of whatever need they had once fulfilled, no doubt for someplace far from here. He wondered what had become of that place.

They had wind driven generators on his planet as well, which is why he was able to recognize them, only he had never seen them so massive or severely built, and not in these numbers. Generally, they were used on his world by rural farmers for the processing of grains or the pumping of water. He had also seen such farms on one particular planet, whose atmosphere produced particularly high winds, used for augmented power supply to drive their conveyance systems, but never for the inscrutable use that he found here. There was an austere beauty to them, however, as if they were still some sort of sentinels to this old way of life; perhaps they had been a clever solution at the time, but now only seemed to indicate a people whose demand for energy had well surpassed their ability to create it.

By the time he came out the other side of the field, it was night. The stars had come, and the moon had risen, which, luckily for him, was nearly full. With the aide of the moonlight, he decided to continue his exploration to the scrabble of rock formations that seemed to connect to the high desert beyond.

* * *

Once up in the highland—and no sooner had he hiked out of view of the fields—than he was surprised to come upon another structure. This one, however, was so small, it nearly blended into the rocks, so much so that he almost passed it without noticing. It was a small wooden cabin. The only thing that betrayed its presence was a warm glow that came from its modest window, and the slight tendril of smoke that emitted from the pipe haphazardly protruding from its roof.

Constant's initial instinct was to go right up to the door to inquire after its inhabitant, but then he remembered Frank informing him about the unspoken agreement that they had with the few remaining inhabitants of this area: they left each other alone. He also remembered their proclivity towards violence against strangers, especially in the interest of protecting their homes. So he decided against an immediate encounter, in the middle of the night no less, which would indubitably startle the dweller within.

Still, he could not bear passing on the opportunity to meet one of the plain's inhabitants, so he decided to wait until morning. Securing his horse, he found a nearby rock and sat upon it with his legs folded, and passed the night in deep meditation.

Chapter 26

The old man
in the desert

The first rays of morning light broke over the far eastern range, washing the hillside clean of the night. Constant awoke still sitting with his legs crossed, slowly stretching his arms to greet the fresh morning air. He breathed it in deeply. The cabin was aflame with the orange light of the new day but did not appear to have been disturbed. The window however no longer glowed and smoke no longer emitted from its chimney. It was placid with the dawn.

Constant stretched in the sun and greeted Cloudfoot with a bag of grain that he had brought with him. He took some water from his canteen for himself and sat back atop the rock to wait. He did not have to wait long.

Soon enough, a wizened old man burst forth from the front door. He was naked from top to bottom, save for a long white beard and heaping wild hair. His body was gnarled, and he was bow-legged, like an old tree, but sprang along the ground with surprising energy and agility. Waving his arms and seemingly speaking to someone or something, he ran along to the back side of the cabin, no doubt to pass the morning's water.

A short time later, he came back around carrying a sloshing wooden bucket of water, still speaking, now shouting to either himself or someone in the cabin. His hair was wet, as he had apparently doused himself in the same source, perhaps a well, that he had filled the bucket from. As he rounded the front he stopped short—he had caught sight of Constant. He stopped speaking and froze for but a moment, looking pointedly at him, but then merely continued on into the cabin, waving and shouting as before, as if nothing had happened.

Constant was uncertain of what to do. It was not clear if he had actually seen him. It was not clear if someone else was in the cabin. It was not clear if the man was even sane. Still, he was fairly sure he had actually seen him, and the very fact that he was not disturbed, nor even seemed to care about Constant's presence, was a good sign that he could approach the man without too much trepidation. The premise of unadulterated Contact with an inhabitant of Egolsia was too much for him to resist. He decided to approach him.

He went to the door and lightly wrapped his knuckles against it, as he knew was the custom. He waited a moment. There was no obvious answer, but he could faintly hear the man still speaking within. He tried again. Still no response. He tried the nob. It was open. Constant did not instinctively sense any danger from this man, so decided to go in.

As he cracked the door and cautiously peered, he could now distinctly hear the man within.

"Yes yes come in. Of course come in. I am familiar with the lights! Yes, yes of course come in…"

Constant was taken aback for a moment. The light was dim—in stark contrast with the now bright sun outside—so it made it difficult to see, but he did perceive the figure of the man inside. His back was to Constant, but he seemed to be talking to him.

"Yes yes come in, of course come in. I am familiar. I am familiar with the lights…"

Without turning around, he waved his bony arm at him to come in. Constant entered the dwelling. It took a moment for his eyes to adjust to the decrease in light. He could see the man hovering above an iron stove top, intently preparing something.

"Yes yes, only a moment. He should sit we'll have it together!"

Constant looked about for who he might be talking to and gave a start. To the left of the stove, atop a wooden furnishing, was the body of a small furry quadruped frozen in mid-stride. It had startled him as he had not perceived the presence of the animal previously, yet there it was. It took him a moment to grasp this creature's significance. It was no longer living. It had been preserved.

The place was much tidier than he expected it to be, even well kept—but perhaps more by its ascetic virtue than one of cleanliness. The furnishings were minimal, but then what filled the space where clutter was not were creatures like—not the same, but of the same state—the one to which the old man had appeared to be speaking. Some big, some small, some furry and fierce, others soft and sublime, but all seemed to be frozen in time as if cast by some spell, fixed by some clever science.

After the shocking initial impression, it quickly became clear to him that these creatures had been mummified for some unknown reason, and perhaps by the inhabitant of this dwelling. It was clear he was speaking to them as they were alive, but in his prudence, Constant decided not to be distracted by the eccentricities of this being. He was to keep focused on his task at hand, which was to get to know this person, and tactfully interview him without himself being revealed.

"I enjoy your 'mummies,'" Constant said to him jovially.

"Yes well, aren't they! Mummies and daddies the lot of them! Sisters and brothers too!" the man replied with his back still turned. "And sons and daughters as well, come to think of it," he added. "Yes well, they do have a lot of opinions don't you know! Yes well, I hear you hear!! He is isn't he!" He seemed to be speaking to them again, but now turned to Constant. "Yes, tea now, hmmm—Mister... Mister..."

"Zeta. Doctor Zeta. I am very pleased to meet you. And may I ask what your name is?"

The old man spun around, nimbly quick and examined him through a squinted eye, hair tasseled in his face. Constant now noticed that he had put on some sort of desert sarong. It was quite colorful, with very intricate patterns.

"Doc-tor it is. Yes well of course. Doctor. We all need healing here I always tell them!"

"Tell who?" Constant asked.

"The dead ones! Don't you see them? Yes well, it's no surprise. I always tell them: Deus ex machina! Deus ex machina! It's already been decided!"

Constant made a move to question the man but was intercepted by a hot cup of brew deftly handed to him by a wiry arm.

"Tea of course. Desert tea. No Spirit in it this morning, don't you worry—that's for when the moon has let Them out. Yes, here in the desert the spirits hide in the shadows during the day. Too bright! Too bright! Yes, yes I said I was familiar with the lights," the man said, again turning his attention to the small mummified quadruped.

"What's his name?" asked Constant, playing along.

"Him? Not sure...," he replied a bit surprised. "It once was Akoaway," he mused "When he lived and roamed the desert high. Then he lost his name when he died, but got another one. I'm not sure what he goes by these days. Good question! Here, let me ask him." He turned back to the still animal. "What is your name?"

Nothing. He again asked very deliberately, very loudly, and waited. "Hmm. No answer. I'm not sure either. I just know him as You! You! You!" He began pointing and shouting "you!" at each of the frozen figures until he had finished the last.

"Now let's get down to it," he said spinning back around, flopping his head into a folded hand. "I know why you're here. Yes, I know very well why you're here. Like I said. Deus ex machina. Deus ex machina. It's all been decided. It's only a matter of time. A time concerned matter. A time concerned matter of time. It's all been decided you see. The question just is, which one is it?"

"Of what?" Constant asked him, trying to follow.

"Which line Doctor, which line of course," he bellowed back.

"Which line of what?" Constant asked him again, perplexed.

"Of time! Of time Doctor, of time. Like I said, it's just a matter of Time. Line." He replied, seemingly satisfied with his answer.

Constant was quite unsure on what level, or to what point, to respond to him on. Was he saying he knew why Constant was there? But that was impossible. Unless he was some sort of mystic or shaman. He had met many in his travels and studies, and some were even stranger than this man. Still, it was entirely possible that he was just intoxicated or crazy. It was most likely the latter, but Constant remained unconvinced.

His eyes fell to the other side of the room. There was a contraption that, by its construction, appeared to be some sort of distillation apparatus.

"Yes yes, you've seen the Spirit. It's how she gets in and how she gets out. Like a sip of the desert, she comes in and lets us out!" he shouted, shaking his hands over his head. "You'll see. Tis no matter of contemplation you will see. She'll crack you open and let you see." He leaned in close to him, almost whispering. "Here here I know why you here. Leave it to me. Like I said I'm familiar with the lights. Deus ex machina. Deus ex machina. That's what I always tell them: It's all been decided."

"Why is it that you think I am here?" Constant asked in earnest, mostly trying to direct the conversation, but still quite curious as to his response.

He paused, then answered him as if he had not heard the question. "But it is no matter in any ways. Like I said. Deus ex machina. The ground's too stained. He'll tell you. Don't worry. He'll tell you. But it's not all for nothing…"

"Tell me what? Who will?" Constant asked, a bit exasperated.

"HE will." He gestured over his shoulder out into the desert, almost mouthing the words. "It's only, the ground is poisoned you see. Stained all white and red and black and now gray. It can't grow any more people—You see. But you shall see! He'll tell you. But it's not all for nothing. Not all for nothing you see. You will see you see. I say you will see!" He cried out and fell silently slumped over his tea, sipping it delicately.

The old man—whom Constant only later realized had never given him his name, and had forgotten to ask again for it—then proceeded to confirm for him categorically each of his suspicions, namely that he was drunk, crazy and probably a mystic. Only, it wasn't clear if he were a shaman who had lost his mind on drink, or a drunk who had imbued himself into a mystic state of mind, or something else altogether. He supposed it did not matter, the result was the same. Or perhaps it was all this time alone, out here in the middle of the loneliest of deserts, with only his dead friends, and the spirits to talk to.

He stayed all day, in intense discourse with his new friend. Once he was able to transcend his manner of speaking they were able to discuss many of the subjects that had been weighing on Constant—they spoke of the fate of the land, the spirits of the desert, and the inevitability of all things. When he finally decided it was time to leave, it was only because he needed to: the sun was beginning to set, and he wanted to get to the sacred rock before nightfall.

Before he departed, the old man insisted on giving him a mixture of dried herbs wrapped in a piece of burlap which he called "desert tea." He handed to Constant very carefully, like a sleeping animal he was scared to awaken, and told him it was for his desert communion. Thanking him, Constant saw himself out.

He greeted Cloudfoot at the stoop of the porch, where he had waited patiently for him for the entirety of the day. He fed him a handful of grain the old man had given him for the purpose. Stroking his nose and whispering, he began to tell his old friend about his new one. He mounted him gingerly, and the two of them rode out together on the tail of the evening sun.

Chapter 27

Constant's
second vision

The twilight seemed to last forever. Constant made his way in a steady but unhurried manner to the sacred rock. The desert tea the old man had given him he had stowed in his pocket and planned to drink that evening. He would wait till the light had gone from the sky, and he would meditate until the moon rose high enough in it to replace the sunlight with its reflected version. He had been wishing to commune with the spirits, and now there was much on his mind.

He was happy, he thought. He had come here with a mission, with a theory he desperately needed to test, and to a large degree he had done just that—but only to a certain extent. It was not exactly how he would liked to have had it, but he had connected with these people, he had made contact in the way he had believed in, and he had shown them another way. And his vision, the creation of the generator, had worked, and it could mean a whole new possibility for the people of this planet. But still, the more he thought about it, the more he found his feelings were mixed.

To start, he was not sure if the Collective was going to agree with him on all of those points. He had found a way around the embargo mainly by the fact that the technology had been developed on the planet, and then secondarily because it could not be directly used for interstellar travel or war. But he knew these were only technicalities at best. Especially the second part, as he admittedly had no way of knowing that the knowledge contained within the generator wouldn't someday lead to the development of something destructive.

More to the point—and here is where the uncertainty of his feelings originated—if his theory had been that if he could create an integrated form of Contact, if he could show them a possible new path that came from their perspective, thus not disrupting their evolutionary flow, then on one level he had done so. Though on another level, he had clearly handed them the answer, something which undermined the central premise of his theory. And moreover, he was not sure the answer he had given them was the right one.

It was still clear that although the beings he had been working with understood, at least to some degree, their culpability for the position they were in, they were still part of a larger collective notion which believed wholeheartedly in a mechanized evolution. That is to say, they thought that if they were able to "figure out" enough technological advances, mostly involving comfort and convenience, then they would ultimately develop a world in which they would all be happy.

Nor did they see the full circle of their own oppression. Oppression is not usually the cause of violence, it is the result of it. Oppression for them was often merely the revenge of a weak power possessor, imagining themselves vindicating the righteous, yet in reality, all the while a slave to nature, filling its abhorrent vacuum with tyranny.

The other false notion was based on the misinterpretation that if enough time passed, their species would evolve past their lower and more violent tendencies. This misunderstanding was typified by the fact that they believed their current form was the biological and psychological end result of their evolution, and not merely the starting point. It was these two points that caused them to be perceived as particularly crazy by the interstellar community, and perhaps even stunted in their mental development.

All these contradictions weighed heavily on Constant, tempering the joy of the previous day's success, as he made his way up the path he had laid to the sacred rock. The last rays of dusk scattered across the vast plain that spread out before the vantage point of his camp as he made his preparations slowly, and with deliberation. The sky began to show its face. The moon started to rise. He made a fire.

Sitting with his legs folded under him, his face washed in the warm light of the fire, he watched the moon climb the broad desert sky. As it neared its height, he prepared the tea the old man had given him and drank it. He waited.

As he had experienced before at this place, he could feel

the invisible spirit of the desert quivering all around him. This time, however, he could feel the influence of the tea—as if another key had been turned, another door opened, another circuit of energy completed, that was now at work. The organic mystery of the land opened up before him.

Out of the corner of his eyes, he could see the Dance of the Helpers, the little creators, the ones who tirelessly constructed the reality of the valley, piece by piece, inhabiting it, moving through it, through the rocks and lizards and cacti, building it, stone by stone, at every moment. They were aware of him, and he of them, and he felt at one with them, as they layer by layer pulled back the veil of the valley, for him to see what lay beneath.

The plain before him glowed in the supernatural moonlight. It was thunderously empty, pregnant, waiting. It was as if it were the innards of some grand instrument, vibrating with a profoundly loud sound that he could not yet quite hear. Suddenly, in the center, a dark red pool began to flow out from nowhere and fill the empty desert floor. It spread out and grew with staggering speed, the deep red, nearly black with night, covering more and more of the dusty white expanse. It quickly reached the edges of the foothills that surrounded the plain, splashing up against them, sending waves back across its surface.

It rose higher and higher, forming for a moment into a dark red macabre sea, a lake of blood glistening in the moonlight. It was a horrifying sight. It swelled and breathed with dark life. Then, as quickly as it had come, it shrank smaller and smaller, seemingly draining into the tiny cracks of the plain, until it was completely absorbed. The desert floor buckled, then contracted and hardened, before turning a glassy and cracked bone white. A figure stepped out in front of him.

He was an extraordinary sight. He was tall, towering well over Constant. He was the same deep red as the rocks in the valley. He seemed to radiate with an array of feathers and hides. His eyes were piercing and profound. They twinkled wildly with the stars.

He did not say a word, but only stared at Constant, communicating at first only with his electric eyes, and then broke the silence with a deep voice in his head:

"This land is stained with the blood of man."

He gestured behind him, and Constant saw a vision of the sun coming up over the dark desert.

"Watch now. Watch the Sun rise and stretch to offer its power to the land. Yet it falls only hot and undrunk on the red-stained rock."

He turned back to Constant. Constant watched.

"This land is stained with the blood of man. It has been bitten and burned by man. This land is stained, and cursed and desolate now. Man poisoned this land with the blood of his brother. He has poisoned himself. He has poisoned this land. Nothing grows here now. He cannot grow new here now. He must be renewed. This land must be renewed."

"Is there anything that can be done?" Constant asked him, with barely a whisper.

"It must be renewed. We must be renewed. The Sacred Hoop must be made whole again. But that is for another time—"

No sooner had these words entered his mind, than the

figure stepped out of view. As soon as he did, the vision of the sun quickly disappeared, and the whole desert floor shivered as a massive crack split the plain open on the far end of the valley. The crack grew rapidly, heading directly toward where Constant sat, opening the whole desert floor up with a massive black chasm. Faster and faster it came until it hit him like a great wall of thunder. Everything went black.

Chapter 28

Disaster

Constant did not awaken until the following morning. The cool touch of a light snow on his face aroused him from his sleep. He had a sinking feeling in his stomach that something was not right. The previous night's experience had been a profound and disturbing one, but that was not solely what was bothering him. He did not feel anything coming directly from Owvi either, but he still had an uneasy feeling that something was off. He broke camp quickly, put an extra blanket on Cloudfoot and departed.

The snow was coming now as only a light flurry, and the Sun was still shining brightly, giving the desert morning a surreal aspect. The whole landscape was cast in that sweet melancholy glow of the sun storm. He rode quickly, clutching the blanket tightly about his shoulders. The temperature had dropped, and the wind had picked up, but the snow stayed steady. He would be back at camp soon enough.

As he reached the ridge that brought the North Camp into view, he saw immediately the giant plume of smoke swelling up from the heart of the camp, and out into the flurrying sky, like an artificial cumulus spun up from the desert floor. Digging his heels into his beloved horse, he leapt forward into a gallop. Though he never took his eyes off the plume, it did not register what was happening until he saw the first flames lick out from their origin. His heart sank. The tower that held the generator was on fire.

His mind raced, trying to grasp the cause—was it an accident? Had it failed? Had the remaining group of bandits or nomads or whatever they were returned for revenge? His eyes scanned the horizon but found no discernible answer. No sooner had he cleared it of the fire's cause, than it was broken by a large, rectangular black shape crossing it on one of the far hills. He looked to the other side of the Grand Mile and saw two more of the same such shapes slip into view.

It was quite difficult to tell exactly what they were. They slid gracefully across the ground, like an anti-gravity airship, but they were not so gracefully shaped—more like elongated cubes, all black with no discernible features. There was something deeply unsettling about their abstract and unclear black nature, moving like light missing from the desert. It was not clear how and if these objects were connected to the fire, but it seemed logical they were. One thing was clear—these were definitely not the bandits, or at least not the ones they knew.

As he got closer, Constant now noticed the commotion going on in camp. A number of people were desperately and unsuccessfully trying to put out the fire. The generator was now consumed with flames. Suddenly, he thought of the dream vision he had seen as he had passed through the wormhole. A swirl of snow, a fuzzy and flickering column of fire, a profound sadness—was this what he had seen? Had this all been destined to happen?

He snapped himself from his revery, as he saw that others in the camp were now scrambling to the very same defensive positions he had seen during the assault by the bandits. His heart was racing. He did not know what to do, so he simply held his position on the hilltop, intently scrutinizing the scene to see if he could grok what was actually happening. It didn't make any sense.

From what he could tell, the strange vehicles had not yet breached the camp, yet something had. Smoldering in the snowy air, two deep pits flamed in the center of camp— perhaps the result of some sort of projectile weapon? Perhaps launched from some great distance? Whatever had caused them, it was no longer visible, and no new ones had appeared. The scene, however, was becoming more clear to him now. They were under attack.

This was no siege for precious resources or asserting territoriality either—whoever or whatever was coming at them meant to destroy them. And totally. The black monoliths that were quickly closing in were bringing death and destruction with them. Constant's heart sank even lower, he did not understand why, but he could feel the intent of harm coming from them, and the despair of an imminent disaster. He dug his heels into Cloudfoot and raced down the hillside, heading as fast as he could toward camp. He must find Dr. Whitney.

No sooner did he reach the edge of the cultivated fields

than one of the massive black destroyers crested the ridge on the far side of camp. It rose up and slammed down heavily, crushing the ridge-line beneath it. It moved as a wheeled terrestrial vehicle, but with the grace that only an anti-gravity augmented craft could manufacture. He could also now see some of the seems in its all black exterior. The anterior portion was defined by some sort of glass front, the side panels tracing out what were possibly access doors, and a top panel that now slid open, allowing a long black tube to rise up out of it. The vehicle ground to halt and the tube pivoted into a new position.

A stream of intense blue light shot forth from it, connecting with the base of a large antenna that sat atop one of the command buildings. The building's roof exploded into flames and the antenna crippled under the heat, crashing down on the structure next to it. This was it. It was pandemonium.

The second destroyer smashed through the front gate at a terrifying speed before skidding to a stop in the center circle. Another tube rose up out of its roof and began ejecting pulses of blue light seemingly at random about it, setting fires, digging smoldering holes, and sending anyone unfortunate enough to be near it screaming and smoking into the air. It was a horrifying sight. They were like rabid, metallic beasts, tearing at anything around them with piercing blue claws of fire and light, flashing out at dizzying speeds. It was truly a nightmare.

Many of the community's defensive guards took up tactical positions and tried to retaliate with return fire. It was to no avail. Whatever they threw at these beasts did not even leave a mark on their polished shells. The tubes suddenly stopped firing, and the doors on their sides slid open. Thin, black metal humanoid-like machines mechanically filed out. Their heads were like flat discs standing on end, with large circular holes in their middles, and their bodies were long and thin and looked deceptively delicate.

This contradiction was made immediately apparent when someone charged the line, firing on one. It sprung madly out of line, stretching half its body length to a new location, like some nightmarish robotic cephalopod. It snapped into place and aimed its odd head at the defending camp member. A deep, thundering thump emitted from its head and a strange ring-like wave passed out from the center of the hole. The pulse slid through the air like a moving heat wave before slamming viciously into the chest of the defending camp member, audibly crushing his bones and sending him to a crumpled heap in the dirt. Everyone stopped with shock, unsure of what to do next.

The humanoid machines wasted no time spreading out, snapping each out of their daze, snatching and binding those who thought to throw themselves to the ground in surrender. Others quickly found that while formidable, the machines were not indestructible, and could be brought down with a well-placed shot, or a heavy blow to their thin necks. And so, the battle had begun.

Constant secured Cloudfoot and quickly began making his way towards the house on the hill. His hopes were that Dr. Whitney and Owvi had fallen back there, like last time, and had not gotten trapped in the bunker. He was not as worried for Stantish, for he knew he could take care of himself, but he needed to ensure that the others were out of harm's way. His mission was clearly over, and now the safety of Dr. Whitney and his team was the only thing of importance. They needed to get out of there, and fast.

Just as he stepped onto the path that led up the hill, one of the machines made its impossible appearance in front of him, stretching in an instant into his line of sight from some other unseen place. Constant braced himself for something terrible to happen. Fortunately, it didn't. No sooner had it snapped into place, towering over him than Stantish flew into the scene from the snowy shadows. With a mighty swing of a fire ax, he separated its deadly head from its ghastly body and dropped it to the floor. It was now that Constant noticed that he himself had fallen to the ground. Stantish rushed to his side.

Stantish bent over him, tears in his eyes. He was OK. He reached up for Stantish just as he heard that sickening thud burst out from somewhere not too far away. Stantish's body jerked as his back was clipped by the sound wave. He hit the ground hard. Constant cried out, leaping over top of him to shield him from any further harm. He looked into his eyes—there was still light in them, but it was fading. Blood trickled from his nose, and Constant caressed his face. He brushed the debris from his braided hair dusted with the dirt of the desert floor. His deep red face whitened. Constant could feel the cold of the snowflakes falling on the back of his neck, but he did not notice himself crying. His friend was dying.

Stantish struggled to speak, and half smiled back at him. "This world, Constant... This world... I..."

"I know Stantish. I know," he paused, stroking his cheek. "I will see you when we both are Light."

Stantish smiled and nodded. He had nothing more to say. The light went out from his eyes.

In the moments that followed, Constant only remembered flashes. The vision of Dr. Whitney and a crew of defenders running across the hillside firing at the machines. The slow motion of the generator, engulfed in flames, falling over behind them. The sight of Princess Fatima's silver and black ship emerging from a cloud of snow, and landing in the field behind them. And then, everything went white.

Chapter 29

Revelation

Constant awoke in a large, white room with sparse white furniture. He sat up quickly, the previous day's event flashing blindingly by his mind's eye. Still dizzy, he took in the room around him. There was a fuzzy group of figures off to the side. Amongst them, he could make out only Dr. Whitney, who sat crouched on the floor with her back against the wall. As soon as she saw Constant awake and looking about the room, she shot up and ran to his side.

"How are you feeling?" she asked, searching his face tenderly.

"I am not harmed. Are you OK? Where's Owvi?" he replied with a shallow breath.

"I'm fine. Not sure where Owvi is. Not sure where anyone is—they split us up from the rest of the group." She dabbed his forehead with the corner of her jacket.

"Stantish is dead," he said heavily.

She looked down and sighed. "I know," she said looking back up at him. "I'm sorry."

"He died in the act of defending me. It was an honorable death for him. He is happy now," Constant replied with a conciliatory tone. She did not buy it. She knew he was devastated by Stantish's death.

He pulled himself up, and they sat looking ahead, holding each other's hand, squeezing the other for comfort.

"What do we do now?" he asked.

"We wait," she said with resolution.

They did not have to wait long. A hidden door in one of the placid white walls slid open and revealed the dark, stately figure of Princess Fatima. She was dressed in a fiery red woven gown, embroidered with tribal patterns, and a silver and black headdress that fanned impressively around her head. She was quite a sight. Flanking her were two officers, wearing the gray and white patterned urban snow fatigues that Dr. Whitney recognized from before. They were standing at attention with long, black tube-like projectile weapons. She smiled and waved them back.

"Dr. Zeta. Dr. Whitney. Please forgive the theatrics. They were necessary to make an impression on all of you," she said in a cordial voice, and her best diplomatic posture— the kind that is supposed to simultaneously put you at ease, and terrify you with its casual nonchalance.

"Theatrics??" Dr. Whitney was already fuming. "People are dead. Our friends are dead," she growled through gritted teeth.

"Yes well, that was unfortunate," the Princess answered without breaking her tone. "We did not expect such resistance from you—that was a bit of a surprise. And the detention drones were also programmed, shall we say, a tad overzealous. We're remedying that now. As for your generator, or whatever it is that you called it—" she paused, striding into the center of the room. She turned to face Constant. "That simply could not do. It had to be destroyed." She waved her hand and resumed her pacing.

"I don't understand," Constant said slowly, suddenly joining the conversation. He seemed dazed by it all, and sincerely confused.

"Ask Dr. Whitney. She made a promise to me that she would keep me informed about your activities. Had she done so, all this might have been avoided," she said, nearly with a hiss.

"I made no such promise." The rage beneath Dr. Whitney's voice now was barely contained by her clamped teeth.

"No matter. It's all the same. You see Dr. Zeta, there is a great deal your people do not understand about our planet, understand about us." The Princess now turned to Constant.

"I came here to understand," Constant retorted pointedly. "I came here to help."

"It was I who brought you here Constant Zeta. It was I who sent your people that message. Don't you understand that? You may have come to understand it, but you were kept in naiveté by your friends here. You see Constant, there are two types of beings on this planet—those that rule, and those that are ruled. The ones that are ruled here, well they are not much more than animals. They are perhaps one or two laws away from total barbarism, and as such they must be contained, they must be controlled. It has always been this way, and it will always be this way. And the way we maintain control is not merely by fear and brutality—that way is, shall we say passé—no, now it is by maintaining comfort, and creating dependence. It's a much better method.

"Fear, intimidation, hatred of a common enemy, while they have worked for the ruling class for many thousands of years, they are not the greatest means of control—they are volatile, and they have their limits. A far better form we have found is addiction, or more eloquently put, 'the promise of a better tomorrow by improving the comforts of today.' Far more potent than the fear of violence, is the fear that their little screens might go off, that the lights might go out. The people of this age are far more interested in the maintenance of their way of life, rather than exactly how they live it. Addiction to comfort, you see, is the ultimate degradation of man. It creates apathy. And now—at this critical time—this has been upended by the disintegration of the longtime government of this nation, and by the chaotic weather and withering of the land, caused by the permanent shift in our weather systems. But you know all this. And then you—you sought to give them solace and to cut us out of the process. US!" Her own voice now starting to boil with anger, her fist unconsciously clenched.

"Dr. Zeta, with all due respect, we simply cannot stand for this. And so, your little machine had to be destroyed," she said haughtily, trying to recompose herself, smoothing her rich dress with her elegant hands.

"Where's Owvi?" Constant interjected.

"Owvi? Your companion? He is fine, don't you worry, he is nearby. It was never our intention to hurt you, mind you. Anyway, I needed to speak with the both of you, and it seemed expedient to do it at the same time. I believe that I already know Dr. Whitney's response, but I do not yet know yours. Now, if you will let me get to my point—" she said curtly, continuing.

"You'll have to understand how we could not allow you to provide any such liberation, any such undermining of the power structure that we have meticulously created over the course of centuries. It once was that nations and civilizations would rise and fall, and their rulers with them. But we have long since divorced ourselves from that baser natural process as well. Now we say, let them crumble— only we will stay standing, and even profit by it. And why shouldn't we? We carry the God-given, hereditary responsibility for the custodianship of this race of man—shouldn't we be compensated?" she snorted. "Besides, it is evolution that dictates that the strong shall flourish, and so we can hardly be blamed for ensuring that the weak stay weaker, so that we may permanently maintain our position. It's simple genetics, you see."

She seemed now very satisfied with the case she laid out but kept going all the same, as if she had remembered some important points after all.

"You see, it is we who control the world, Dr. Zeta, and we will continue to do so. We are the only ones equipped to do it. If the means of control requires the control of energy, then we shall have it. If it's oil, then it means oil. If it means water, then water… but you see Dr. Zeta, it is all a balance. We harbor no ill will towards our people. And as shepherds, we want our sheep to be as comfortable as possible. That's where you come in."

"I'm offering an opportunity, Dr. Zeta—an opportunity to do good. I want to give you a job. It is why you came here is it not? I want you to come with me, and help us find a way that we may provide the energy that we need to sustain life on our planet, but in a way that is more reasonable, so that we may continue to govern properly—and profit by it—as we always have.

"Listen, we have no desire for the continuance of a culture of war on this planet—I assure you myself and those I work with find it a nasty and distasteful business and would love nothing better than to eliminate it. Unfortunately, there are others within my peers who believe it to still be a necessary evil. Nevertheless, everything is moving away from that, so I promise you that whatever you help us create not only will not be used for violence but will actually help us to ensure a future with no war."

She paused and leveled a perfect smile at Constant. "You see—there it is. You can help us achieve peace."

"Think Dr. Zeta," she continued, "it's what you always dreamed of: a chance to use your theory of Contact to change the fate of an entire planet. Let's see your doubters argue with you then. Of course, you can remain anonymous if you wish that too—your people do not even know you are still alive. Your ship just left our orbit this morning. You are all alone. Come now, join us."

She ended with a heaving smile. Her beautiful hand elegantly outstretched, waiting for his. Constant simply stared at her and did not move or speak. They both stood there frozen for more than a moment, then finally, he spoke.

"I will consider it," Constant replied.

Dr. Whitney shot him a hot glance of disbelief, her eyes as large as moons. The Princess's eyes grew large as well, and she returned to him a sickeningly sweet smile.

"Good Dr. Zeta, very good. I must say I am impressed by your broad vision." She turned to Dr. Whitney.

"Dr. Whitney, I will give you the same benefit of the doubt that your intelligence will require the same consideration as Dr. Zeta's. We leave in the morning. I will expect your answer by then."

Dr. Whitney only stared at the floor, shaking her head darkly. Constant watched as the Princess gracefully turned and glided to the door. She made a subtle gesture, and the door obediently slid open so she could leave. As she exited, Constant caught a glimpse deeper down into the hall where a number of individuals were gathered waiting for her, talking amongst each other. First, he noticed two humans dressed in all black Egolsian suits—they may have been Egolsian as well, but something was strange about their demeanor—but that was not what caught his eye the most. Standing with them were two OoCulays, perhaps even one of the ones he had seen at the underground conference building so many days back. Sensing his gaze, one turned to look at him as the door slid shut.

Dr. Whitney turned to him as soon as it closed.

"You can't be serious," she smoldered.

He turned and met her gaze.

"No, of course not. You know, I have managed to retain some understanding while here on your planet—I believe you call this tactic 'lying,'" he said with a smile.

"What are we going to do?" she asked, unsure herself.

"I don't exactly know, but we only have tonight to do it. Let's talk."

They moved away from the others, off into one of the bright white corners, and whispered to each other their plans for escape.

Chapter 30

Escape

It did not take long for Constant to establish mental contact with Owvi. He had felt his presence on the ship since he had awoken, but had not been able to precisely determine where he was. After some discussion, they were able to estimate where they were in relation to each other. Owvi was with Tii, and a small group of other people, in a similar such room, but one that appeared to function for stowage. Based on the size and what they knew of the layout of the ship, they deduced that they were on the same level, and perhaps only two rooms away from each other.

The plan they then conceived proceeded thus: Constant believed the hand gesture he had seen the Princess use to open and close the doors was not necessarily replicable by them, as it most likely included the scan of some visual signature of her hand—but it might by Owvi. He also believed there would be some override for the purposes of an emergency evacuation of the ship, as in the case of fire, or some other distress. This meant that if they were to employ this means of escape, they would not be able to free themselves clandestinely, but rather would have to attempt to slip away under the screen of chaos.

In the process, Constant and Owvi strategized, Owvi would attempt to provide some disablement or other to deter the Princess's guards from pursuit, or at least give them long enough to put plenty of distance between them and their pursuers. The plan was not perfect, but it could work—it had to work. They would surely not be going with the Princess, and if they did not comply it seemed certain that, based on the Princess's veiled threats—and her decree that they were in fact already considered dead—that they would not live to see the next sunrise. And so, they waited until the midpoint of the night, when the ship seemed quietest, and put their plan into action.

Constant and Dr. Whitney waited on either side of their door for Owvi to override the system. The other crew in Owvi's room waited patiently as well. Tii was to lead them out as, and much to her displeasure, Owvi was to fall back and go in the opposite direction. The hope was that he could find a more significant electrical access point than he had in the room, in order wreak as much havoc upon their computer systems as he could, so as to give them all as much of a head start as possible.

Owvi stood at the front of his group, with the others breathlessly filed behind him. As he gestured at the door, he concentrated on the mechanism that was programmed to read it. The scene was almost comical, and—because of the high pressure of the situation—one of the engineers tried to suppress a nervous laugh. This immediately drew stern looks and hushes from the others. Finally, the absurd display paid off. There was a hiss, and the door sprang open, immediately followed by a bright flashing light and a high pitched tone. Without hesitation, Tii moved them quickly out of the room.

Constant and Dr. Whitney heard first the tone, then braced themselves as their door flew open. They cautiously looked out down the hallway. There was an intense blinking light, and an alarm that seemed to come from nowhere, but they could neither see nor hear anyone else. It appeared they had been wrong about where they thought they were positioned in relation to Owvi. Exchanging glances, they moved out into the corridor, trying to orient themselves.

No sooner had they stepped out into the hallway, however, than Constant heard the staccato sound of boots coming up behind them. He spun around to meet one of the camouflaged soldiers running up to him holding his weapon. He braced for confrontation, unconsciously placing his arm in front of Dr. Whitney.

"Dr. Zeta! Don't be alarmed—we need to briefly evacuate the ship. There appears to be some malfunction. I need you to head this way with me," he told him with urgency. Exchanging a look, Constant and his group nodded and followed him. They were unsure of their next move but were now resigned to play it all the way through.

As they neared the rear of the ship, they could hear the commotion of the crew running about, most likely in some procedure to check out the status of the ship, and verify whether there was, in fact, a fire. It seemed there was some confusion though, as lights began to flicker. Perhaps Owvi had made it to the right control panel and successfully added to the chaos.

Finally rounding the last corner, they could feel the cold of the outside air rush by them. A large aperture in the floor had opened and gave way to long ramp that disappeared out into the swirling white snow of the harsh black night. They could hear others outside, and silently rejoiced when they came into view, as they were quickly escorted out into the night's air. They all stood there, not knowing exactly what their next move was, but alive with the electricity of their potential escape.

The moment was short-lived, however, as the gangway was darkened by a silhouette angrily shouting down to the few guards that had joined them below. It was an officer, and he was furiously ordering his subordinates to 'get them back in here!' and 'who told you to let them outside!' and a multitude of other expletives. There was a moment of terror amongst the group. One of the captives started to back away, looking for an opening to go. A soldier promptly raised his weapon and shouted at him to not move. The screaming between all of them escalated, and then, all of a sudden, it stopped.

The officer at the doorway, and all the ones he had been yelling at, including the one with the gun, had all frozen. They had each suddenly been overcome with a horrible, debilitating feeling. The officer experienced what felt like a pinching sensation at the back of his neck, and was paralyzed with the terrible experience of the profound violence of his life. The young man at the end of rampway vomited out of repulsion but was unable to move, and so was not able to keep it from lancing on the front of his fatigues. The group, unsure of what was happening, stood and stared. The cause soon revealed itself: Owvi appeared at the top of the ramp, silhouetted by the light.

He wasted no time and hurried down the ramp. Tii immediately sprinted toward him. He had given them an opening and was now emphatically gesturing for them to take it. Before they could, however, there was a crack, and a pink mist exploded from the foreheads of one of the female camp engineers. She sank to her knees. Dr. Whitney grabbed Constant by the arm and pulled him into the night. Everyone else in the group made a run for it, dispersing into chaos.

Another set of figures had darkened the doorway. Streaks of red light lit up the gangway, flashing over the heads of those in the group attempting to flee into the night. One streak grazed Owvi's arm, and he faltered. Tii ran around in front of him like an angry bull ready take anything meant for him. A soldier charged down the ramp pointing his weapon at her face, but as soon as he reached her, the fire in her eye instinctively made him hesitate, just for a moment. It was this hesitation that saved her life and cost him his.

The side of his head exploded, and blood and tissue splashed wildly into the air, catching a few of them in its spray. Tii turned to see the soldier who had vomited on himself standing there with his weapon raised, pointed at where the now expired soldier's head had been. He then only looked at them before he took his weapon, placed it under his own chin and discharged it. Tii screamed.

More figures were now coming down the plank, but they

did not wait to see who they were. They picked each other up and ran out into the blinding snow. They could hear the ringing of the weapon fire grow dimmer the further they ran away. Shadows passed chaotically through the white, some fell, others did not, and the flashes of projectiles faded into the pale of the night.

Fates Unknown

Chapter 31

A road away

It was a stark, bright day. The hills were cast in that alien light that follows a traumatic event—it seems to have no care for what just happened, but is still fully conscious of it, in some far away way—somehow indifferent, yet still all knowing, cold, and illuminating. The transport skidded across the languishing desert, dust clouds lazily drifting from its trail. No one inside it spoke.

Tii was in the back nursing Owvi's wound. Constant sat in the driver's seat, with Dr. Whitney co-piloting next to him. They were heading toward a rendezvous with some of Dr. Whitney's resistance contacts. They were trying to find a way to get out of the country. First, however, they were heading to a place that was safe, a place with sympathetic people, and they were just going to have to figure it out from there.

They traveled a pale white three days before finally reaching a refuge in the arid mountains of the southwest of the continent. It was a secluded place known locally as the

Valley of No Name. By the time they got there, they were numb and exhausted—they had spent the last few days trying to digest and recover from the strange and horrifying events they had just witnessed. It was night, and they were lead to their quarters in a haze of exhaustion.

When morning came, they were able to see all the magnificence that was the mountain range in which they were now couched. The refuge itself was wholly embedded in the interior of the mountain. However, there was a series of grand terraces carved out of the rock face that were not visible from the ground, nor from above, due to their careful construction. The clever architecture so allowed a nearly unobstructed, nearly invisible view of the great range and the sky that hung above it. It was there they sat all day, as they tirelessly met with a number of Dr. Whitney's liaisons.

They learned of Frank's escape and of Ambassador Able's betrayal. Frank and a few others had apparently gotten free right as the rest of them had been captured. Their intelligence told them that the camp had been thoroughly ransacked before it had been ultimately dismantled. Some structures had even been completely burned until there were only ashes left. According to their communication from Frank, this was not before one of the engineers, Hayward, was able to transmit a photo-electric version of the plans for the generator to a globally networked computer system. This was no small feat. The community had in the end been a failed experiment, but perhaps that knowledge they had so briefly brought to life there could live on and someday redeem itself—if it were to get into the right hands.

The report on Ambassador Able was not clear. It was

not clear whether he had been in contact with the Princess prior to her arrival at the camp, or had in any way contributed to the reason for her ultimately going there, but one thing was for sure is that when her ship finally left, he went with it. The whole business was dark and dirty. And that was not all. War had broken out in North America.

It was more than one war really, dozens in fact. Everyone was fighting each other. That complicated things for them even further, as it would only become more and more difficult to travel now. They were only able to spend a few days in their mountain refuge before they would have to leave again. It was just enough time to conceive of a plan and arrange their next move—but not enough for the recovery they so desperately deserved.

They had been granted access to a special community that lived in a remote location in the central part of the continent. Even Dr. Whitney's weighty influence had not purchased their invitation; it was Constant's. There was little discussion of whether to go and who would go. They were a unit now. They would all go together.

Before they could leave, however, they had to spend a few days more at the refuge while they negotiated a complex and clandestine travel plan. It would be a winding and severe journey, to say the least, with an exhaustive series of outmoded forms of transportation and double backing, but it was a route that they could not afford to have traced. They all contemplated it heavily. It was a possibility for a whole new beginning for them there on Egolsia—a chance they needed to take.

Chapter 32

The desert flower

Tii stood in the doorway, watching Owvi on the veranda quietly looking out over the vast desert below. She had been told that the terraces which perforated the rocky faces of the refuge had been designed in such a way that satellites could not detect them from above, but still, him standing so close to the edge made her terribly uneasy. They were all most definitely being looked for.

She was sure that he knew she was there—he always did—but he made no move to show it. He simply stood there, taking in the air with his signature quiet contemplation. Sometimes it seemed like he knew what she was going to do before even she did, so she rarely surprised him. Tii supposed some might find this unsettling, but she did not. She liked it. It made her feel connected, understood. She had recently realized that she had actually felt misunderstood her entire life and not even known it until she had met this man—this being—who did. And now, she knew just how much this meant to her. It was everything.

He reminded her of that folk tale her Grandfather had told her as a little girl. He said that in this world, there was one major difference between Heaven and Hell. In Hell, everyone was gathered at a large table, full of food yet no one's arms could bend as they had no elbows. Everyone tried to eat, but every clumsy attempt ended in frustration, and as a result they all starved with sustenance right there in front of them, just outside of their reach. Heaven, he said, was much the same. Everyone sat at another large table, also full of food. They too could not bend their arms as they had no elbows. However there, unlike in Hell, they all fed each other. For her, Owvi was Heaven. He fed her, and she could tell she fed him too.

A breeze gently whipped through the veranda, into the open door, bringing with it the chill of the desert morning air. Instinctively, she wrapped the silk that hung about her shoulders around her arms and stepped out into the open air of the balcony. She breathed in its fresh scent and walked up slowly behind Owvi, placing her head softly on his shoulder and her hand gently on his wound.

"How is it?" she asked.

He turned his face towards her and smiled softly. "It is fine." He turned his gaze back toward the desert, and they held each other in silence.

"It's beautiful isn't it?" he said, regarding the vast arid plain before them, bordered by a hazy blue range on its far side. She agreed.

They stood there for a moment, pressed gently against each other, imbibing the harsh beauty of the valley. For them it was a moment of much-needed respite; the last few days had been difficult ones to say the least. They had seen their creation, their labor of love, destroyed right before their eyes, for reasons that even Tii—a native Egolsian—struggled to comprehend. They had fled their temporary home amidst a storm of violence. Stantish was dead.

Despite all of this, however, they could not consider their endeavor a complete failure. They had found each other, they had found real love. Their paths, they both felt, were just opening up for them, not closing, not narrowing, not coming to an end. It was a new way for them, and despite their sadness and exhaustion, they were both electric with the feeling of it.

For Tii, her hereditary feelings of being bound to this planet had all been cut. She knew that they could eventually find a way to leave if they so desired, but her and Owvi had decided to stay for now; they both intuited that there was more for them to discover here. Besides, Constant and Sarah were both staying, and though Owvi and Tii were not necessarily bound to Egolsia, they felt strongly that they were bound to them.

"Someone told me of a particularly remarkable flower that grows in the desert. For years it stays hidden in the plant, weathering all kinds of hardships, before it finally, mysteriously grows. Have you heard of this?" Tii said, breaking the silence.

Owvi, turned, intrigued. "No, I have not, but what a poetic gesture on the plant's part," he mused.

"Yeah," she continued. "Some say it's the most beautiful and singular flower in the desert." She paused, thinking of something else. "I know we must leave soon, but I wish we could spend more time in this place. It's so pretty, and there sits this beautiful desert, just out of reach… and I have this odd feeling we will never be back this way."

He turned to her and smiled his smile meant just for her. She supposed she should have learned by now that vocalizing a wish in front of Owvi often came with a response. She did not have time to finish this thought, however, before he turned to her and placed his thumb on her forehead, on the spot right between her eyes.

The next moment she found herself feeling very large, spreading out all across the valley. Owvi was with her this time. She couldn't see him exactly, but she experienced his presence acutely. They were at the same time as wide as the valley and yet also swimming through it. The valley floor and all of its flora was lit with a strange, eerie light that seemed to pulse around its edges. All of the planet life was breathing together, and she with it. And then she saw the flower.

It was alive. It shivered brightly with its own inner light. She communicated this to Owvi, but in a manner she had never done so before. It was as if she had placed the meaning of her thought in his mind before she even thought it. Previously, she had heard the thoughts in her mind, the words, as if someone was speaking to her, but this was different. This was the transmission of meaning before a thought of it was even formed—like some sort of proto-thought. It was wild.

She did not remember how long they spent in the desert together, playing reverently amongst the mountains, but when they finally returned to their room, she slept the whole night with a peace that she had not felt for a very long time. The image of the flower danced in her mind, keeping her company in her dreams.

Following the day, after only a brief taste of respite, they finalized the preparations for their journey. Without further ceremony, and in the quiet of night, together they all departed.

Chapter 33

New beginnings

Constant struggled to keep his grip as the antique transport bounced and clanked through the muddy waters, grinding its way across the river bed. Everyone was sore and bruised from the road, red and cracked from the rays of beating sun. They were making their way hazily through the thick green jungle, all hot and wet all the way through, on roads that almost seemed designed to impede travel rather than facilitate it.

The group had been traveling for what seemed an endless number of days before they had gotten even close to what felt like striking distance. It had been slow going, the entirety of the way. The war was making travel difficult, and the means they employed to keep their progress from being noticed made it even slower. But now that they were almost there, exhausted and nearly demoralized, they felt the closeness of their aim.

They finally had to leave their vehicle when the road was swallowed entirely by the relentless jungle. From there they had to cut their way through what seemed an eternity of twisting vines, broad wet leaves, and a confusion of monkey howls and rustling in the bush, to the point where, after almost a week, they were not sure if they had made any real progress. There was a clear access road to their destination, but they had been instructed not to use it, a fact which made their slow process seem all the more cruel. Within these parts, the community they were traveling towards was not a secret. They had friendly relations with their surrounding neighbors, but Constant and his team's identity was too valuable, too hot, to risk even one loose tongue.

On the last day, they cut their way from sun up all through the heat of the day, until almost evening, when finally they slashed through the last wall of vegetation. They stumbled unceremoniously out into a clearing and collapsed onto the close-shorn grass. They found themselves on a great lawn, crisscrossed by footpaths, and illuminated by the bright, equatorial light. They just lay there, exhausted and unsure of which way to go. Dr. Whitney knew they were expected, but not necessarily the when and how, and they had surely missed the main entrance. All the same, the sun was warm, and it was nice to not be hacking through the stubborn bush anymore. They sat up to catch their breath.

A slight shadow fell over them—a young woman had quietly appeared on the path without them knowing. She addressed the dazed travelers.

"Constant Zeta? Sarah Whitney? And you must be Owvi and Tii? Hello and welcome—my name is Lu. We have been expecting you. Come, you must be hot and tired. This way—come, come," she prodded them, marking their stupefied state.

They all stood up and numbly followed behind her. Taking one of the narrow footpaths through the shade and shadows of the sizeable broad-leaved palm trees, they soon took a turn out into an even grander lawn, around which the entire town spread itself out before them. The cool breeze and serene setting had begun to wake them up. As they walked through it they all took note of its pleasantly geometric layout—the order was oddly calming. Later they found out the plan was, in fact, a transposed version of the ancient grounds that lay buried beneath it.

Buzzing with a variety of activity, much of the town was evidently still under construction. All of the finished structures they saw seemed to be still quite new, and there was also a number that looked to be temporary, made of banded limbs. By the look of the architecture of those huts, and what was ostensibly being laid down as permanent, it appeared as if they were making use of both traditional and modern methods. It all made for an eclectic but oddly cohesive aesthetic tone that none of them had seen before.

The buildings were nearly all of circular composition, with a clay and limestone base, and an upper wooden structure that allowed light and airflow, which in turn supported a shingle or thatched roof, depending on the size and permanence of the structure. It was impressive to see the repetition of this dome-like shape, newly laid out and composed in half concentric circles that radiated out from the center of the town. They were apparently heading in that direction.

As they made their way, they paused in the broad central square. There they saw ahead of them a more angular series of structures. The first were two very long tube-like buildings, with dome-like ends, that flanked the central structure in the center circle of the town. In between them stood an enormous building which looked like it was composed partly of a new construction and partly of the truncated base of a much older pyramid. Lu told them it was the foundation of a temple that once existed there and was part of the ruins upon which the town now sat.

Apparently, the town itself was raised up quite a bit from the surrounding forest floor, lifted by an invisible lattice of buried rock, layered eon upon forgotten eon. And it was at the center of all of this that they had erected this new structure, also of limestone and wood, also a place of communion for the entire community. Constant could not get over his impression of the town. The entirety of the village was a humbly beautiful site. He squeezed Sarah's hand, and she squeezed back, letting him know she was feeling much the same.

Their survey of the grounds ended when they were shown to their modest but quite clean quarters, where they were able to unload the little they had packed, and finally rid themselves of their road worn and jungle drenched clothes. Lu had attendants bring them fresh clothes and linen, and they were shown to a large outdoor bath where they spent the rest of the day refreshing themselves, in the cold water and warm sun, washing away their long and tedious journey.

The grip of fear and apprehension that had hung over them for so many days had finally begun to dissolve. The horror and genuine pain of having their highest hopes dashed and destroyed, while watching so many of their comrades die for the most inscrutable of reasons, had put their morale at a desperate low. As for Constant, he could not form any distinct regret for his coming to this planet, for this had in fact been the ultimate opportunity to test his ideas, but he was now laid bare and devastated. His conception of the nature of humanity, and of himself for that matter, had been completely disintegrated. Still, he had hope. He watched Sarah warming herself in the sunlight, the light playing on her skin like some ecstatic painting, and he experienced a certain happiness he had never felt before. She turned and looked at him. Her eyes were warm and shone brightly with love.

* * *

That night after they were heartily fed, they were shown to the central temple where they were to finally meet the leaders of the community. Lu led them there through the town's winding pathways, paved with crushed seashells that glowed in the moonlight. It was quieter now in the dark than it was during the buzz of the daylight, when much of the community had been out and about, heartily pursuing the tasks of the day. Now, however, they could hear laughter and singing coming from one of the long public structures, whose windows were warmly illuminated by the firelight inside.

Sarah too was glowing, Constant remarked to himself, as they walked hand in hand. They were both wearing tan and white, thin woolen tunics, as many in the town did, which shone in the pale light. Owvi and Tii followed behind them, quietly drinking in their surroundings. There was a peace here—a relaxed, but somehow still focused atmosphere that was as infectious as it was palpable.

Lu led them up the worn steps of the old temple. Behind them, they could see the blue washed tips of the trees of the grand, sprawling jungle that surrounded them. It was quite a magnificent sight. She took them back through a newer series of arbors deep within the compound, where the whole structure opened out into a large, open air pavilion, surrounded by a serene cultivated garden. At the center of it all was a grand tent, warmly illuminated by torches, and populated with several shadowy figures. As they approached down the garden path, a vivid scene unfolded before them.

A thin white gauze hung about the roof of the tent, flickering in the torchlight. The interior was furnished with three large low platform beds, and a few scattered stools, all of which were richly covered in layers upon layers of brightly dyed woven blankets. Upon these several women were reclining, all wearing their own version of the white woolen tunic, some draped with bright yellow and red scarves, others modest and simple. One was playing some sort of string instrument, as the others listened and laid on pillows, propped up by their elbows. On the middle platform, three more women sat cross-legged and appeared to be presiding over the rest. They all made quite an exquisite scene sitting there together, but the woman who sat in the center of it created the most striking image of all.

Her skin was deep red, which was accentuated by her bright white robe. Her hair was long and blue black, braided at the top, with wildflowers tucked behind her ears. She was smaller of frame, yet appeared larger than life against the rest of them. As Lu stepped up to the tent, they all calmly rose to greet them.

Without a word, the woman who they assumed was their leader, walked directly up to Constant, took his hands and kissed them. She looked at him with a warm, bright smile.

"Constant Zeta. I'm so happy you are here. My name is Itzel."

She turned to Sarah.

"And Sarah. Sarah, I'm so happy you too are here."

She took Sarah's hands and kissed them as she did with Constant. She greeted Owvi and Tii in the same fashion and then introduced all of the others. Constant and Dr. Whitney both expressed their gratitude for her assistance in bringing them to this place, but she quickly waved her hand and invited them to sit, returning to her previous position. When everyone was settled and had taken their seats, she spoke.

"I know there is much to talk about, and I know you have come very far, and although I have already been told some of your story, I am quite eager to hear it from you. But first—I'm sure you would rather hear something from us?" Constant and Sarah both nodded in mute affirmation. She flashed her eyes in return and continued.

"I am assuming you know very little of us, as we prefer less to be known of us outside the bounds of this community. Although Lu has given you some introduction, I asked her to allow me the pleasure of telling you about what exactly our aim is here, in this place that you have now found yourselves.

"I will get to the point. It is our aim here to found an entirely new society—and we have chosen this very land upon which to do it. We have all come here from many different, dying and splintered nations, in an attempt to create a whole new way of living—one that is as great as the ones of so many years ago—but one that is not in any way founded on violence.

"It is not equality we seek here, but empathy. Freedom from violence. We believe the demand for equality is solely an aspect of a rule of law where empathy has failed. There can be no violence where there is empathy, where there is real brotherhood and sisterhood. You see, for us, there is no more important nor profound pursuit than the eradication of violence from ourselves, from our society, and from the very heart of mankind."

"It is not some lofty utopia that we aim to create here either. We do not believe a utopia is possible here on Earth, at least not as long as there is war all around us. As long as there are those who are suffering. As long as we are all who we are. We feel that it is just not possible—but we do believe it is within our reach to found a lasting civilization that does not require the genocide or exploitation of another people. We do not think that kind of culture can be a lasting one—that kind is one that will someday be eroded by the very violence that it was founded upon, even if it does contain profound or altruistic tenets. We've been there—as they say—and done that. A thousand miles to the north of us is the decomposing remains of one such nation. It is necessary for us to start over, and we do not wish to make the same mistakes again.

"And so, Constant Zeta, when we heard of your work with Sarah and her colleagues, and what was the subsequent outcome of that, we were more than happy to have you come here and take refuge with us. You may stay as long as you like, and who knows, perhaps we will be able to be of some service to each other." She smiled and sat back contently, patient to hear their response. Two of the women whispered between themselves.

Constant, still a bit bedraggled from the journey, could not help feeling a bit of irony in all this. He had come to this planet with the imagination that he could somehow change it, somehow help these people from their insanity—but now he had seen the foolishness of this, and had been feeling the humbling sting of this realization ever since that final, fateful night at the North Camp. And now—now—now was that moment of Contact that he had so many times dreamt of in his private thoughts: a hand outstretched, but this time perhaps it was he that needed the help…

While Constant was caught in his reverie, Sarah broke in with her own response. "Though I cannot help to believe I know my friend's mind here—I can only speak for myself when I say that we all come here mostly empty-handed, save perhaps for a bit of hard won experience. And our love for each other." She squeezed Constant's hand. "But whatever we can do to help—"

Constant nodded in affirmation and replied. "Itzel. You cannot imagine how long I have waited patiently for this, how many times I have composed my words for just such a moment. You might even say that so far it has been my life's work. But now I am at a loss for those words. I can only say that this meeting is perhaps an opportunity for both of us. Whatever I can do to help, but I am no longer on this planet to teach—I am here to learn, to live. I am here to understand."

Itzel smiled back. "Good then. I'm sure we'll have more to talk about in due time—and I am sure I will hear more from your friends as well," she said gesturing to Owvi and Tii who, still sat silently behind them, seemingly more interested in each other than the profound moment unfolding in front of them.

"But for now—" She motioned to someone in the shadows. In a moment, the tent was filled with trays of food and flasks of wine. Someone began playing the music they had heard when they had first walked up.

Constant felt hope. Maybe there was something for him here. Here on this planet, here in this place. It was a chance for him to not just think, not just observe, but to Be. Here, he could really live, and perhaps grow to understand the essence of humanity. He knew he was no longer here to try to change anything, but maybe by really living he could be a part of the transformation Egolsia so desperately needed—and in the process perhaps find his own true purpose. Someone tapped him on the shoulder, breaking his reflections, and offered him a cup of wine. He took it happily.

And so they spent the night with them there talking, and laughing, and singing together as new friends do, and the stars passed slowly overhead.

www.ingramcontent.com/pod-product-compliance
Lightning Source LLC
Chambersburg PA
CBHW071545110726
47908CB00007B/2004